"Hello?" Leah said eagerly.

A few seconds of silence elapsed before a male voice said, "Is Alexandra there?"

"Alexandra!" Leah gasped before she could stop herself. Then, clearing her throat, she said more calmly, "Alex has gone to bed. Can I take a message?"

"This is her friend," the man said. "Is this Leah Stephenson?"

"How did you know my name?" Leah demanded with a combination of anger and dread. "Who are you? Why are you calling here so late at night?"

"You leave message for me then!" the man said. He had a strong Russian accent that Leah hadn't noticed at first.

"Look, you—" Leah began.

"You tell Miss Sorokin she meet me tomorrow, three P.M. sharp."

"Where?" Leah asked shrilly.

"Alexandra knows where," the voice said coldly. "You must tell her when." Then there was a click, and Leah knew he had hung up.

The SATIN SLIPPERS Series
By Elizabeth Bernard
Published by Fawcett Girls Only Books:

Other titles in the Girls Only series
available upon request

STEPPING OUT

Satin Slippers #8

Elizabeth Bernard

FAWCETT GIRLS ONLY • NEW YORK

RLI: $\dfrac{\text{VL 7 \& up}}{\text{IL 8 \& up}}$

A Fawcett Girls Only Book
Published by Ballantine Books
Copyright © 1988 by Cloverdale Press, Inc.

Library of Congress Catalog Card Number: 88-91296

ISBN 0-449-14544-1

Manufactured in the United States of America

First Edition: January 1989

With special thanks to K.D. Dids, Gilda Marx-Body, Capezio by
Balletmakers, Taffys, and Marika Bodywear.

*To Nate and Zachary, whose dancing
keeps me on my toes*

Chapter 1

Leah Stephenson leaned against the barre in the Red Studio on the second floor of the San Francisco Ballet Academy. Gently, she dabbed at her damp forehead and shoulders with the towel she'd just pulled from her bright blue dance bag. Leah was tired, but she knew the special Saturday rehearsal for their upcoming week-long performance of *The Nutcracker* was not over.

The mid-December sky outside the tall ballet studio windows was pitch black. But the clock above the door said it wasn't quite five yet, and rehearsal was scheduled to last until six. Leah knew from past experience that Patrick Hogan, *The Nutcracker*'s choreographer, would not dismiss them a second early.

"I'm sure I don't need to remind you people that Monday is our first full cast rehearsal," sandy-haired Patrick, an accomplished danseur himself, said when their five-minute break was over. Anxiously, he paced up and down the line of weary dance students. "Everything we've been working on needs more work before you're ready to dance with professionals," he added, referring to his fellow members of the Bay Area Ballet Company.

Finally, stopping in front of petite, dark-haired

Kay Larkin, Patrick said, "We'll begin with Kay's solo in the first act, since that's new."

Leah was glad that her good friend Kay had won the part of Clara. Seeing the happy look on Kay's face these days made it nearly impossible for Leah to feel jealous. As it was turning out, Patrick's Clara was custom made for Kay's sparkling allegro work. And at this point, Leah was just glad she would be dancing in a major production with the Bay Area Ballet at all. Leah was dancing only in the corps de ballet, but it was her own fault she'd missed out on the audition for the role of Clara.

First of all, Leah had allowed her short-lived modeling career to take precedence over rehearsing diligently for the audition. Then, when it came time for the actual audition, Leah had missed it. Furthermore, Leah had been distracted by the chance to appear in a movie with her ex-partner James Cummings and her friend Andrei Levintoff. In the end, she had turned down the film role—but it had still kept her from auditioning for *The Nutcracker.*

Never again, Leah said to herself as she watched Kay marking the steps of her solo dance with Patrick. For now, developing her skills as a dancer was more important than being in the spotlight. Though Leah knew she'd never model again, she didn't want to rule out the possibility of starring in a dance-oriented Hollywood movie ... but not until she'd finished high school at SFBA. Leah still had so much to learn!

"Kenny!" Patrick said, gesturing for Kenny Rotolo to join him. Kenny would dance the part of Clara's younger brother Fritz, once Patrick finished marking Kay's solo with her. "I want to ease into the solo with Fritz's little boastful dance, dancing full out this time with Robert's piano. Listen to the music but don't forget to count," he said. Then Patrick rapped out the beat on the top of the Red Studio's baby grand piano. The accompanist Robert joined in on Patrick's fourth measure of tapping.

As the music began, Kay lifted her head, and Leah could see her transforming herself into the eager Clara. Kenny strutted about the room, doing chaîné turns, acting like the perfect show-off. He continued to move with more and more boldness, first performing a jêté, then a tour en l'air, as he demanded to be the center of attention. Finally, stealing the shoe Kay clutched, Kenny spun away from Kay and performed his violence on the poor nutcracker. Then he dropped the shoe and danced away.

Tenderly, Kay scooped up the shoe and began the solo Patrick had added to the choreography. As Clara, Kay danced her sometimes romantic, sometimes childish solo with the poor, wounded nutcracker. Leah was captivated by her friend's ability to make the fantasy world of *The Nutcracker* seem real. Kay was so exciting to watch, so utterly believable as Clara, that Leah was completely won over.

Finally, Kay swept down in an arabesque penchée as she gently tucked the shoe beneath an imaginary Christmas tree. Spellbound, Leah was able to see both the nutcracker with its poor, wounded jaw and the dazzling tree in the Stahlbaums' parlor. Kay had performed magic! Her expressive dancing had made everything real.

When Kay's solo was over, Leah led the other

students in a round of enthusiastic applause. For a moment, Kay looked as if she were waking from a dream.

Patrick smiled. "Better," he said, giving Kay a reassuring nod. "In fact, very good! Now we'll try the corps' entering dance." Clapping his hands, Patrick said, "All right couples, take your places."

Unfortunately, Leah had such a terrible time with the simple corps dance that she was afraid she was throwing everyone else off. She even managed to step on the heel of the girl in front of her. Mercifully, Patrick didn't single Leah out for a scolding when the dance was over. Leah decided Patrick must know how physically and mentally drained she was from the combined ordeals of the week before.

"It's ten after six, gang," was all Patrick said. "So, as they say at the movies, 'Th-th-that's all, folks!' " Patrick concluded, doing a perfect imitation of Porky Pig and successfully causing the class to laugh with him. As the laughter subsided, the students gave Patrick his customary round of warm applause.

Leah walked to the back of the studio to pick up her dance bag. She was determined that come Monday, she would be her old self again, well rested and ready to dance her best.

"Wait, people!" Patrick suddenly said. "Before you escape, I have an assignment for you." There were a few groans, but Patrick merely cleared his throat loudly and went on.

"Your assignment is to let loose! Enjoy yourselves! A moment ago you were all acting as if you'd never even *been* to a party. Your steps should have been light and anticipatory, not heavy and tight. You need to party, people. On Monday, I want to be able to believe that you're actually going to a party at the Stahlbaums' house!" With that, Patrick turned from the puzzled-looking students and walked to the piano, where he began reviewing *The Nutcracker* music with Robert.

Students began picking up the odds and ends they had dropped about the room, leg warmers, sweaters, sweatshirts, shawls, and dance bags. Leah noticed a few of the boys standing over by the windows, discussing something in loud whispers. Briefly, Leah considered going over to see what the fuss was all about. But all she really cared about at the moment was getting back to Mrs. Hanson's boardinghouse and soaking in a hot bath.

As she walked down the corridor to the girls' dressing room, Leah began to wonder how she was going to have the kind of fun Patrick had just assigned. It was nearly six-thirty and, as far as Leah knew, no one had planned a party. Anyway, Leah was so tired that she doubted she could manage going to a party even if there was one. Maybe Patrick just meant that they should catch the spirit of partying, or something like that.

"Now I *know* Patrick Hogan is nuts," Pamela Hunter, the fiery redhead from Atlanta, appeared to be saying to her own reflection in the mirror as Leah entered the dressing room. "First this weird, overdanced version of *The Nutcracker* with a solo for Clara in the first act, and now this strange assignment. Where in the world does Patrick expect us to find a party to go to? If this were Atlanta, there would be hundreds of parties to choose from. But this place," Pam said, making a disparaging gesture that clearly included the Academy and probably all of San Francisco as well, "is a social wasteland!"

Leah was tempted to tell Pam she was the one who was crazy for preferring Atlanta to the wonderful San Francisco Ballet Academy. Leah loved her hometown of San Lorenzo, California, too, but there was no way she preferred it to the Academy.

Leah knew, though, that starting something with Pam just wouldn't be worth the grief. Leah had had run-ins with Pam before, and Leah knew that fighting with the overly ambitious Pam was anything but fun.

As she released her long blond hair from its faltering chignon, Leah bit her lip to keep herself from saying anything. With her large blue eyes focused downward, Leah began digging for the purple plastic brush she kept in her dance bag. Once she'd found it, Leah began the arduous task of detangling her waist-long golden mane.

"I think Patrick was just telling us to relax. He was probably telling himself to relax as well. Patrick has been as jumpy as Leah's cat Misha lately," one of Leah's friends, Katrina Gray, offered. "And that isn't like him."

"It seems to me Patrick's got good reason to be nervous. He's been tampering with a classic!" Abigail Handhardt, one of Pam's few friends, commented in a disapproving tone of voice.

"Tampering is right, Abby," Pam huffed, raking a comb through the waves of her thick auburn hair, her green eyes flashing angrily at her own reflection. "I was Clara back home three years in a row," she added. "So I know what being Clara is all about. In fact, the review I got claimed I was a ballerina at eleven years old."

"Who was the reviewer, luv?" Finola Darling, an exchange student from the Royal Ballet School in England, asked. "Your mum?"

"My point is," Pam said, deliberately turning her back on Finola, "Patrick is trying too hard. *The Nutcracker* doesn't need all the embellishments Patrick's giving it."

Leah was just about to leap to Patrick's defense when Alexandra Sorokin rose majestically from the bench where she'd been sitting and said, "For once I must agree with Pam."

Leah's mouth fell open in surprise. She still wanted to defend Patrick, to say that Kay's dancing was brilliant thanks to Patrick's interesting choreography. But Leah and Alex had recently had a misunderstanding that had seriously jeopardized their friendship. Disagreeing with Alex about *The Nutcracker* didn't seem worth the risk of upsetting Leah's Russian friend all over again.

Still, Leah was puzzled. It was no secret to anyone, including Pam herself, that Alex wasn't exactly a fan of Pam's. Why, Leah wondered, was she siding with Pam now?

"Patrick," Alex went on as she picked up her jet black dance bag, "tries too hard to make something out of nothing, to, how is it said, make a sow's ear out of a silk purse?"

"You mean make a silk purse out of a sow's ear," Kay said, walking into the dressing room just in time to correct Alex's mixed-up expression. "What are you guys talking about, anyway?"

"Nutcracker," Alex quickly replied. Then, turning to Leah, she said, "You know what I am saying,

do you not, Leah? *Nutcracker* is not a ballet like *Swan Lake* or *Giselle.* The best dancing part in *Nutcracker* is that of the Sugar Plum Fairy! But that, I think, is why Patrick has used this music for two dances."

"You're wrong if you think you're agreeing with *me,* Sorokin," Pam said defensively. "I think *The Nutcracker* is a wonderful ballet. It's Patrick's *version* I don't care for."

"If you knew dance history, Pamela, you would know everyone connected with *Nutcracker* agrees with me, including Tchaikovsky. So, you see, your *small* opinion does not matter," Alex said haughtily as she started toward the dressing room door.

Before opening the door, Alex turned back and glared at Pam with her sensuous, almond-shaped eyes. "Even you, Pamela, must know that ballet companies like your company in Atlanta put on *Nutcracker* so that people like your parents and your grandparents and all your friends will spend money to see people like you move about the stage. *Nutcracker* was, is, and always will be a fund-raising event, a recital for children!"

Leah looked anxiously at Kay. She was afraid that Alex was so caught up in angrily putting down Pam that she wasn't aware she was also criticizing Kay. Kay was busily taking the lamb's wool off her big toe and didn't appear to be listening to the argument going on around her. But that didn't mean Kay's feelings weren't hurt. Kay, Leah had learned, was very good at hiding her feelings.

Finally, unable to keep silent any longer for Kay's sake, Leah said, "Patrick is trying to change that, Alex. In fact, I think Patrick *has* changed that. Everything from Kay's chaînés to Kay's bourrées made me believe in Patrick's revisions. Kay was Clara, and Clara was beautiful!"

The normal rosy flush on Kay's cheeks darkened at Leah's compliment. Looking up from her sore toe, Kay said, "I felt like Patrick's Clara that time, too. I really did. I'm glad you could see that, Leah," Kay added, her deep blue eyes sparkling brightly with affection for her friend. Leah returned Kay's smile, pleased she'd spoken up like she had.

"Everyone is entitled to her opinion, I guess," Alex said, sounding angry, and not just at Pam, either. Leah was about to ask Alex if something more than *The Nutcracker* was bothering her, but before she could, Alex threw open the dressing room door and strode out.

"What was that all about?" Pam asked Abigail. Abigail shrugged and the two of them left together, whispering to each other on their way out.

Leah continued to work on her hair as other girls drifted out of the dressing room.

"Patrick was very receptive to a couple of changes I suggested just now," Kay told Leah once the two girls had the dressing room to themselves. "I was amazed. He really listened to me!"

"I'm not surprised," Leah said. "I'm sure Patrick knows how interested you are in choreography. Besides, Patrick is one of the easier instructors to work with around here—much easier than Christopher Robson was when we did *Swan Lake* with him!"

"I agree, but Patrick isn't really what I wanted to tell you about." Kay's blue eyes twinkled like they did whenever she had a juicy piece of gossip to pass along, which was quite frequently.

"It's not?" Leah said, slinging her dance bag over her shoulder.

Kay shook her head. "No, it's not. While I was waiting to talk to Patrick after rehearsal, I noticed that the boys were pretty excited about something. They were still talking by the windows when I left the studio."

Leah laughed. "You always think someone is up to something, Kay," she teased. "The boys were probably plotting to grab a hamburger together later or something."

Kay shrugged. "Maybe. But if that was all there was to the laughing and back-slapping that was going on, I doubt if they would have clammed up as soon as I got within earshot of them."

"They probably know your reputation as the biggest gossip at SFBA," Leah said, giving Kay a friendly wink to let her know she was just kidding. As Kay gathered up her things and joined Leah at the door, Leah added, "Come on. Let's get back to Mrs. Hanson's before every drop of hot water is gone. I might die if I don't get to at least rinse off."

Once Leah and Kay were outside the Victorian mansion that housed the ballet academy, Leah slowed down the pace a little. "Before we get back to Mrs. Hanson's, there's something I'd like to talk to you about."

"Sure. What is it?" Kay asked pleasantly.

"First you have to promise not to tell anyone what I'm about to say," Leah said.

Kay covered her heart with her hand. "I promise. I don't blab *everything*, you know."

Leah nodded. "I just wanted to be sure that you knew it was important not to talk about this to anyone else. I want to know what you think about Alex," she said.

"I think she's a terrific dancer and a wonderful friend," Kay replied. "Why do you ask?"

"I don't mean that. I'm talking about the funny way Alex was acting in the dressing room just now. She was so down on everything. It's as if something's really bothering her. Do you know what it can be? Has Alex or anyone else said anything to you?" Leah asked.

Kay reached up and ran her hand through her curly brown hair. "No one's said anything to *me*, but I guess I do know what you mean. Alex has seemed kind of depressed lately. At first I thought it was that movie role you were offered. But even after you turned the movie down, Alex was still upset."

Leah nodded. "I know she wanted me to recommend her for the role instead of Diana Chang. But she said she wasn't mad at me when I didn't."

"Maybe she's sad because the holidays are coming up," Kay suggested. "She told me once that she never goes anywhere during winter break. Her parents are usually touring."

Leah brightened. "I bet you're right, Kay! And if that's all it is, Alex can come to San Lorenzo with me. I'm sure my mother would love to have her." Having Alex around, Leah suspected, would be good for her and her mother, too. Ever since Leah's father had died the Christmas holidays were kind of sad at the Stephensons' house.

"It's only a guess," Kay reminded Leah as they

climbed the steps to the front door of the boardinghouse.

"But a *good* guess," Leah assured her, pulling
the big front door open and motioning Kay to
enter first. "I'm going to talk to Alex about coming home with me for the holidays as soon as I
get the chance."

As the door closed behind Leah, Pam came out
of her first floor room wearing a white satin robe.
"Well, it's off to the bath for me!" she said gaily
as she swept by them, carrying all sorts of bottles
and exotic-looking jars.

"I''m glad there's a bathroom on the third floor,"
Leah said with a sigh. "Otherwise I'd never get to
take a bath."

"No kidding," Kay agreed. "Pam stays in there
so long, I'm surprised her skin doesn't dissolve."

Leah giggled as they started up the stairs. Once
they'd reached the second floor, Kay said good-
bye and headed into the room she and Linda
Howe shared. Leah started up the next flight of
stairs to her room, but before she'd gone more
than two steps, she turned back. Now, Leah decided, was as good a time as any to talk to Alex
about coming to San Lorenzo for Christmas.

Seeing that her door was slightly ajar, Leah
peeked through the crack to make sure Alex was
at home.

"Looking for something?" a throaty voice with
a Russian accent demanded.

"Oh, Alex!" Leah cried, spinning around to find
her friend directly behind her. Alex was in the
midst of her weekly green-clay face mask and hot
oil hair treatment ritual, and she looked nothing
like her usual, beautiful self. "You scared me!"

"That's why I rushed back here after rehearsals," Alex said, slipping past Leah into her bedroom. "I wanted to finish this before you came home. I do not like to be seen wearing a mask. It frightens people."

Laughing, Leah said, "I've seen you look like that too many times to let it scare me, Alex. What I meant was that you startled me."

"I startled you outside my own room?" Alex asked incredulously. "Why were you looking in there, anyway?"

Leah felt herself blush. "I was just trying to see if you were around. I want to talk to you."

Alex shrugged. "I am finished with talk about *Nutcracker,* if that is what you want to talk about. I am entitled to my opinion, am I not, even if it is not the popular one?"

"Of course you are," Leah agreed. "But *Nutcracker* isn't what I wanted to talk about, anyway. I wanted to—" But before Leah could finish, she was interrupted by the sound of a door slamming downstairs and raucous male voices in the front hall.

Chapter 2

"*That sounds like Kenny Rotolo,*" Leah exclaimed, moving to the door of Alex's bedroom. The sounds coming from the first floor of the boardinghouse grew increasingly louder. "And Michael Litvak."

"You are right, it does sound like Kenny and Michael. What are they doing here?" Alex wondered out loud. She stepped into the hall, and Leah followed.

"Girls!" Mrs. Hanson called, her voice punctuated by the sound of her heavy footsteps starting up the stairs to the second floor. "Attention, girls!"

"What's going on?" Kay asked as she and Linda came out of their room.

"A couple of the boys are downstairs to take you to a come-as-you-are party. They said you had to go because of some assignment you were all given after rehearsal," Mrs. Hanson explained, looking confused. "Anyway, they said you'd understand. They wanted to come up here themselves to get you, but I wouldn't let them, of course."

"What did I tell you, Leah!" Kay cried, leaping across the hall to join Alex and Leah. "The boys *were* up to something—planning a party! Come on," Kay ordered, grabbing Leah and Alex by the hand and motioning Linda to join in as she began dancing them around in a circle. "We're going to have fun!"

"You must go on without me," Alex said, taking her hand away from Kay. "I am not going to a party like this." Alex tried to slip past Leah and back into the haven of her room.

"Oh, no," Leah said, blocking Alex's way. "You heard Mrs. Hanson. This is a come-as-you-are party." Leah pointed to the green-clay mask on Alex's face and Alex's oiled hair. "This is how you are, Alex, so this is how you have to go to the party. That's the rule."

"Leah is right," Linda seconded. "You've been caught, Sorokin, and you have no choice in the matter. Either you come along peacefully, or we'll be forced to drag you."

"I am *not* going to this party," Alex said firmly, but Leah noticed there was a mischievous twinkle in Alex's dark eyes. Leah knew that her Russian friend loved parties just as much as Kay did, and it would be hard for her to stay home while they had all the fun.

"Of course you're coming," Leah insisted, deciding that Alex just needed to be coaxed. "You have to!"

Kay nodded. "Come-as-you-are parties are a time-honored all-American tradition. Right, Linda?"

"Right!" the willowy black girl agreed. "Look at me, Alex. I'm wearing this ratty old T-shirt and these silly slippers," Linda added, pointing at her feet which were covered by slippers that resembled a fuzzy bear's feet, complete with claws.

"Yes, but you look cute," Alex pointed out. "I look awful."

"Hurry up, girls!" Kenny Rotolo called up the stairs. "We're ready to roll down here!"

Without allowing Alex to say another word, Leah and Kay hustled her down the stairs with Linda leading the way.

"Eek!" Kenny exclaimed when he saw Alex. "What is *that*?"

"*That*," said Kay, giggling, "is the beautiful Alexandra Sorokin in the throes of her weekly beauty treatment."

"Alex? Is that really Alex?" Michael demanded, leaning close to the Russian girl and peering at her green face.

"Beauty," Alex told the boys coolly, her back ramrod straight and her head regally erect, "has its price."

"Did I hear someone out here mention beauty?" a voice with a lilting southern accent asked from across the living room.

Everyone turned around. Pam stood in the doorway to her room, looking radiant in her white satin robe, her freshly washed red hair cascading luxuriously about her shoulders. Her makeup, as usual, was heavily and expertly applied. Leah had a feeling that Pam had somehow found out about the party in advance.

"You've caught me in my robe, boys," Pam complained, tossing her hair flirtatiously over her shoulder as she sashayed across the room to join the group. Abby followed Pam, looking a little like a small dog following its owner, Leah noted.

"What price did *your* beauty have?" Kay asked

Pam pointedly. Everyone but Pam and Abby laughed.

"I beg your pardon?" Pam said, raising her pencil-thin eyebrows innocently.

"Never mind," Kay said, shaking her head.

Pam looked like she was about to say something else, but before she could, Michael whooped, "All right then! Let's get this party rolling!"

Fitting everyone into Michael's little red car reminded Leah of a circus act in which an endless stream of clowns climbed out of a tiny car. Only this time the clowns were piling into, not out of, the car.

"Move over, Alex," Pam whined once the car doors had been shut and everyone was inside. "You're wrinkling my robe!"

"Nothing would please me more than to get farther from you," Alex assured Pam. "Unfortunately, I cannot move another inch without falling out of the car."

"Hang in there, girls," Kenny urged them. "I know you're crowded, but we don't have much farther to go now."

Michael downshifted his little red compact and shot up the steep hill in front of them. Riding with Michael around hilly San Francisco, Leah reflected, was like riding a roller coaster.

"Here we are," Michael said at last, pulling to the curb in front of the Lydgates' stately gray Victorian mansion where both Kenny and Michael boarded. As Leah got out of the car and examined the house, she decided it was like something out of a fairy tale with its tower and its tall, thin windows. She'd been in the house a few times, but she felt just as impressed by the imposing structure as she had been the first time she'd seen it.

"Remember what you always say to me," Leah whispered as Alex joined her on the sidewalk in front of the house. "Pam isn't worth getting upset about. We're here to have fun, remember?"

Instead of realizing the wisdom in her own advice, Alex merely gave Leah a withering glance. "I am *not* upset about Pam," she declared through clenched teeth. "It takes more than the witch from Atlanta to upset Alexandra Sorokin!" With that, Alex stormed up the brick walkway.

Alex's tone made Leah pause before going after her. What was Alex upset about now, Leah wondered. It had to be more than just the gunk on her face and hair, and Leah hurried to catch up with Alex to find out what was wrong.

But just then Michael Litvak appeared at her side. "May I?" he said, offering Leah his arm just as he'd done several times that day during *Nutcracker* rehearsals.

Leah smiled and took Michael's arm. Together they entered the Lydgate mansion and proceeded to the room from which all the noise was coming.

The first thing Leah noticed upon entering the room was the Lydgates' enormous Christmas tree. Standing in the corner of the room, it was dripping with tinsel and covered by white lights that sparkled like tiny stars.

"Oh, Michael!" Leah cried. "It's so beautiful!"

Michael laughed. "You're a genuine romantic, Leah Stephenson."

Leah felt herself blush. Taking her hand from Michael's arm, she thought about arguing that point, but she couldn't. Michael was right. She *was* an incurable romantic. Furthermore, it was Leah's romantic nature that made her as dedicated to the world of ballet as she was. Everything about ballet was romantic. Unfortunately, being a ballet dancer required such an incredible amount of Leah's time and energy that all of the romance in her life so far consisted of dancing.

"You've assembled quite a crowd, Michael," Leah finally said. Looking around the lavishly decorated room, Leah saw several SFBA students busily setting up refreshments. A couple of things in particular caught Leah's eye: a bowl of iced shrimp, both her favorite and the favorite of her little orange cat, Misha; and a beautiful crystal plate heaped with miniature eclairs, tiny cream puffs, and other fattening sweets usually forbidden to dancers, who had to be extremely careful about their weight at all times.

"We're expecting a lot more people," Michael told her. "Several members of the company are coming, too, I hope."

"Come on, Michael. Let's go over there and see if we can help," Leah said. Forgetting all about smoothing Alex's ruffled feathers for the moment, Leah took Michael by the hand, and together they crossed the room.

"Look at all this great food!" Leah said, stopping by the shrimp bowl. "I haven't had anything to eat today except a carton of yogurt and an apple."

Sauntering over, Kay laughed. "Just looking at this spread is going to make me gain five pounds."

"Forget calories tonight, girls," Don Bryson, a third-year student at the Academy, told them as he set a tray of assorted fresh fruit on the table next to the shrimp. "You can always diet tomorrow."

"That's easy for you to say, Bryson," Michael said, joining them. "I'm the one that usually has to partner Leah in pas de deux class."

"Oh, Michael!" Kay said, batting her thick dark lashes at him. "You mean you can actually *lift* Leah clear off the ground? Here," she added, reaching toward his arm, "let me feel your muscles."

"You can laugh all you want, Kay," Michael said good-naturedly as Kay squeezed his arm and pretended to swoon. "But carrying you girls around and making it look easy is plenty hard."

"And I'm about to make it harder," Leah told him. With that, she turned and, plucking a tiny eclair from the dessert plate, popped it into her mouth.

Soon everyone was sampling a little of this and a little of that. Meanwhile, more party guests continued to arrive.

"Did Patrick convince you guys to have this party?" Kay asked after a moment.

"No," Michael answered. "This party was actually Ben Lydgate's idea. Patrick's little assignment merely convinced Kenny and me to turn it into a come-as-you-are party. We decided it would be more fun this way." Michael laughed. "And we did catch a few people, didn't we?"

"Who's Ben Lydgate?" Linda asked, reaching for a cluster of grapes from the tray Don had set on the table earlier.

"The Lydgates' son," Michael explained. "He's a sophomore at college in Oregon. He came home to study for finals and thought that since his parents had the house all decorated for the holidays, it would be fun to throw a big party for SFBA students and whatever company members we could round up. In fact, Ben was the one who provided the food."

"Ben's got great taste in that department!" Kay said enthusiastically, taking yet another tiny cream puff and putting it on her plate. "Where is he, anyway? I'd like to meet him."

"Don, let's go find him," Michael said. "We'll be right back."

"Poor Alex!" Katrina said, coming over to the girls just seconds after Michael and Don had walked off to find Ben Lydgate. "She's hiding in that corner over there, and she looks as if she'd like to shrivel up and disappear. I tried to talk her into coming over here for some food with me, but she said she wasn't hungry."

Leah laughed in spite of herself. "I think Alex will survive. I saw Andrei come in with Diana Chang a moment ago. Andrei was wearing one of his silly sweatshirts, and Diana was actually wearing pajamas with feet! Maybe Alex will feel better when she sees them. Besides, look at me," Leah added. "I'm hardly dressed for a fancy party like this."

"Where's Michael run off to?" Kay demanded. "I thought he was going to bring Ben Lydgate over to meet us."

"I met Ben a minute ago," Katrina told the girls, nodding toward the fireplace, where Leah saw Pam chatting with a handsome boy who looked about eighteen or nineteen years old. He had nearly white-blond hair and electric blue eyes and he was laughing delightedly. Pam was obviously making her best effort to devastate him with her charm. "He's being entertained by Miss Pamela," Katrina said.

"Did Pam know the Lydgates' son before to-night?" Leah wondered aloud.

Katrina shrugged. "She might have, I guess. The Lydgates are big contributors to the Bay Area Ballet, as well as being a host family for SFBA students."

"Meanwhile, Alex is over there," Kay said, drawing Leah's attention to the other side of the room, where Alex was huddled in a corner by herself. "Doesn't this remind you of *Swan Lake*?"

"*Swan Lake*?" Linda repeated. "In what way?"

"Well," Kay began, "there's Pam, the perfect Black Swan in disguise, and there's poor Alex, the perfect White Swan, enchanted to look like ... like ..."

"Excuse me," Leah said while Kay was still trying to think of the perfect word to describe Alex's green face and oiled hair. "I'm going to go rescue Alex. I think it's time to let her at least wash her face." But before Leah could make it across the room, the noise level of the party suddenly seemed to drop, allowing one voice to rise above all the rest.

"So where is Alexandra Sorokin?" Turning around, Leah saw that the voice belonged to Ben, who was walking across the room with Michael.

"Hey, Alex!" Michael yelled across the room. "I have someone here who's dying to meet you!"

Suddenly everyone, including Leah, turned and looked at Alex. Leah suspected that Alex would gladly disappear through a trapdoor in the floor—if only there were one.

Looking back at Ben, Leah saw him focus his

dreamy blue eyes clearly on Alex. Now that Kay had mentioned it, Ben did resemble Prince Siegfried discovering Odette for the first time. The room remained silent. Everyone's attention, it seemed, was focused on Ben and Alex: it was almost as if they were onstage in front of an audience.

Slowly, as though there were no one else in the room, Ben made his way toward Alex. He was wearing a neat pair of charcoal-gray slacks and a bright red sweater. As he passed a vase of deep red roses on top of the Lydgates' black lacquered grand piano, Ben paused to take one.

"For you," Ben said, his face breaking into a wonderful smile as he stopped in front of Alex and handed her the rose. Even with Alex looking the way she did, Leah could see what a wonderful contrast her dark beauty made with Ben's fair-haired good looks. It was the same kind of contrast that the dark-haired James Cummings had made with blond-haired, blue-eyed Leah before he'd been forced to leave SFBA earlier that year.

Leah found herself thinking what a perfect dance partner Ben would make for Alex. Around six feet tall, he was just the right height for her. A glance at Alex told Leah that Ben's gesture of friendship had really flustered her. With her eyes cast downward, Alex reached for the flower.

"I'm Ben Lydgate," Ben said, his hand lingering on the stem of the rose for a moment so that it looked as if the two were timidly holding hands. Then, as he finally withdrew his hand, Ben added, "I've wanted to meet you for a long time. I've seen you dance."

Ben sounded so romantic and so sincere despite Alex's appearance that Leah could easily understand why a few people started laughing again. Ben's face colored with embarrassment as he seemed to realize for the first time that everyone at the party was listening to his one-way conversation with Alex.

Leah thought that surely Alex would think of something to say to rescue her and Ben from an embarrassing situation. Leah knew from experience that Alex was awfully good at saving awkward moments.

But then all at once Andrei appeared at Alex's side. Putting his arm around Alex in a comradely fashion, he said, "Do you not think you must wash away this green? If that stays on your face too long, the color might become permanent. You will look like someone from another planet!" Andrei laughed, and slowly everyone in the room joined in, giggling at Andrei's joke. Even Ben couldn't stifle a chuckle.

Alex pulled angrily away from Andrei. "Find someone else to laugh at, Mr. Levintoff!" she cried. Then, dropping the red rose on the floor at Ben's feet, Alex fled across the living room.

Chapter 3

Determined to help Alex pull herself together, Leah followed her friend out of the party room and into a short hall that led to the Lydgates' kitchen. There was only one room along the hall, and the door to that room was shut.

"Alex?" Leah whispered, gently knocking on the closed door. There was no answer, but she could hear water running on the other side of the door. "Come on, it's me, Leah. Let me in."

"Go away," Alex said. From the sound of Alex's voice, Leah could tell she had been crying.

"I won't go away," Leah said firmly. Then, trying the doorknob, Leah discovered that the door was unlocked. "I'm coming in."

"Does not anyone in this place respect me?" Alex demanded as soon as Leah had shut the door behind herself.

Leah shook her head. "They weren't being disrespectful out there, Alex. They were only having fun. Their laughter might have *seemed* mean to you, but I'm sure no one meant it that way."

"I'm not talking about that," Alex said fiercely through her tears. "I'm talking about you. I asked you not to come in here, yet here you are!"

"I came to help you get cleaned up," Leah insisted. "I'm your friend, remember?"

"You have not acted like much of a friend lately." Alex shook her finger at Leah. Then she bent over the sink and began splashing water on her face. Her clay mask started to dissolve, coloring the small shell-shaped enamel sink green as it did.

"I'm sorry," Leah said, pulling a small black guest towel from the rack next to her and holding it out to Alex. "I guess Kay and I made a mistake forcing you to come to the party tonight without letting you clean up first. But I never dreamed there'd be anyone as handsome as Ben Lydgate here." Leah couldn't help smiling as she remembered the way Ben had looked at Alex. "He's obviously interested in you, Alex."

"*Interested* in me!" Alex practically screamed. She spun around from the sink and glared at Leah, and the water on her face dripped onto the front of her black sweatshirt. "That boy was just making fun of me, like Andrei and everyone else. He laughed at me!"

"You're getting yourself all wet!" Leah protested, shoving the hand towel into Alex's hands.

"If you are the friend you say you are, you will help me get out of this house. I may not be beautiful like you and Diana Chang, but I am not willing to be a joke." Alex frowned as she took the towel from Leah.

"But you *are* beautiful, Alex," Leah protested. "You're probably the most beautiful girl at this party. I could tell that Ben Lydgate thought so, too. Didn't you hear him say he especially wanted to meet *you*?"

"Meet me so he could laugh at me," Alex said sullenly as she patted her face dry.

"I know you're mad at me," Leah said. "I guess I don't blame you, either. I made you come to this party. But I want to make it up to you. Let me help you get cleaned up."

Alex nodded, her almond-shaped eyes flashing with renewed anger. "Oh, I see. You help me after I am humiliated in front of everyone and we are instantly good friends again? You take my friendship too much for granted, I think."

"Now, wait a minute, Alex," Leah said, feeling her cheeks flush with anger. "First of all, this come-as-you-are party wasn't *my* idea. It was Kenny and Michael's idea. And I wasn't the only one who wanted you to come with your green-clay mask on—Kay and Linda thought it would be funny, too. Plus, it was Andrei who made the joke Ben and everyone laughed at. It was Andrei's *joke,* not you, that they were laughing at. I just happen to be here now because I thought we were friends and because I thought you needed me. But if you don't want my help, if you want only to blame me for things that aren't my fault, I'll gladly leave you here to your own misery! You're full of yourself, Sorokin! But you know that, don't you?"

"And you are not full of yourself, Leah Stephenson?" Alex countered. "I spilled my heart out to you a few days ago. Either you did not listen or you do not care. Either way, you were *not* a good friend then, and you are not a good friend now. Every time you do or say some thoughtless thing, you say you are sorry, and every time I am supposed to forgive you. Then everything goes back to normal." Alex turned away from Leah and began to examine her oiled hair in the mirror.

"Real life doesn't work like that," Alex continued, turning around and looking Leah in the eye. "This is not a rehearsal for a ballet, Leah. I do not care to keep playing the same scene over and over again with you in real life. It is neither fun nor interesting."

Planting her hands on her hips, Leah said, "I don't even know what night you're talking about, Alex."

Alex sighed. "I am talking about the night we talked in your room. The night I told you that I was weary of the dance world. When I told you that I would accept an offer to star in a Hollywood movie if such an offer were given to me."

"But you said you weren't angry with me about that," Leah reminded her. "You know I didn't really think before I recommended Diana Chang for the role of Cara Dean in *Temptations*. And the other night at Cocoa-Nuts you said you weren't mad. Now you're telling me you are. We may be playing the same scene over and over again, but it's not at all my fault!" Leah concluded.

"Can't we get off this movie stuff, Alex?" Leah pleaded. "I'm sorry I didn't recommend you when I turned down the role. I guess Diana was on my mind because Diana was the one who was mentioned in that gossip column in the newspaper. Now, knowing what it meant to you, I wish I had, I really do. But I honestly don't think that it would have made any difference to the producer anyway. He must have been thinking of Diana all along."

"Yes." Alex nodded her head sadly, all the anger apparently drained out of her. "Diana is a beautiful dancer and a beautiful girl, too."

"Will you please stop saying that? You're beautiful, and you know it. Now, wait here," Leah ordered. "All you really need is to wash your hair. Then you'll look sensational, and we can—"

"Forget my hair," Alex said, examining herself in the mirror once again. "Forget the party. If you are my friend as you say you are, you will call a cab for me and get me out of this disaster."

Leah shook her head. "I *am* your friend! But I won't call you a cab. I will help you pull yourself together, though, so you can go back to the party. There's a guy out there, a really cute guy, who might even be able to give your career a boost. At least Pam seems to think Ben has that kind of power. The Lydgates are patrons of the Bay Area Company, you know. I don't know if you noticed, but Pam was pulling out all the stops to get Ben Lydgate to notice *her*. Still, he only had eyes for you!"

"Ben Lydgate!" Alex fumed, her face clouding over. "He was either making fun of me or he is a fool! No boy gives attention like that to a girl with a green face. I looked ugly, yet he acted as if I looked beautiful. He was mocking me!"

"Maybe you *did* look beautiful to him. Anyway, you're being too sensitive. I think you ought to give Ben another chance."

"And if I don't?" Alex demanded.

Leah shrugged. "If you don't, I guess you'll be stuck in this bathroom forever."

"This is blackmail," Alex said, narrowing her eyes to look at Leah. But this time her dark eyes

were twinkling, and Leah knew Alex was no longer
so upset.

"Hang on," Leah said, "and I'll be right back
with some shampoo and some dry clothes for
you."

In record time Leah located Michael and told
him what was going on. He brought Leah some
shampoo as well as a stack of clothes for Alex to
borrow.

"Leah?" Alex said sheepishly when Leah returned with the things Michael had given her. "I
know I told you not to do me any more favors,
but thanks. If you did not help me, I would be
stuck in here, as you say, for a long time."

Impulsively, Leah reached for her friend and
gave her a quick hug. "Anytime," Leah assured
Alex. "After all, what are friends for? You can
wash your hair here or Michael said you could
use the shower upstairs if you thought it was
easier."

"Take a shower here? That would be too much
trouble," Alex insisted.

"It's as easy as climbing the back stairs at the
end of the hall," Leah replied.

Covering her head with a second black hand
towel, Alex said, "Once again, you have convinced
me. Lead the way, please."

Slowly opening the bathroom door, Leah made
sure no one was lurking in the hallway. Then she
motioned for Alex to follow her. Quietly, the girls
sneaked up the back stairs.

Once Alex had showered, she made it clear
that she wasn't too happy about the idea of wearing Michael's clothes. But Leah argued that with

her just-washed hair and her glowing face, it wouldn't matter what Alex was wearing.

Alex still seemed skeptical. "You're the one who got me into this mess in the first place. I'm not sure whether I should trust you or not!" she said, her dark eyes narrowed suspiciously.

"Look," Leah said, patiently spreading out the black jeans and black turtleneck that Michael had given her. "These clothes are great. And Michael even threw in these," Leah added, handing Alex a pair of white suspenders.

"All right!" Alex said, finally smiling. "Remind me to compliment Michael on his taste. I might even take him with me to shop sometime." After their laughter had died down, Alex got dressed.

The black jeans were a little long and a little loose, but with the black turtleneck and the white suspenders, they were completely Alex's style.

"You look sensational!" Leah exclaimed.

Wrinkling her nose, Alex said, "But I have no makeup with me."

Leah shrugged. "I don't have any makeup on either."

"But you never wear any makeup," Alex pointed out. "I, on the other hand, feel naked without mine." Then, plugging in the hair dryer that Michael had given Leah, Alex said with a sigh, "But what can be done? I'll come down as soon as I get my hair dry. You go on."

Suddenly Leah remembered how hungry she'd been. "All right," she agreed. "But if you're not down in ten minutes, I'm sending Kenny and his henchmen up here to get you."

"I'll be done," Alex assured her.

"There you are!' Kay cried as Leah made her way to the refreshment table. "How's Alex?"

"Just fine." Leah took a plate and helped herself to some of the jumbo shelled shrimp. "She's washing up and putting on some clothes. I guess being seen in public like that was too much for her. You know how proud she is." Grabbing an extra napkin, Leah wrapped up a shrimp for Misha, her cat.

Kay nodded. "Speaking of proud, get a load of Pam over there, hanging all over Ben again. I suppose she feels she really put one over on us since she's the only one here dressed for a party."

Leah watched Pam for a moment. She almost had to admire the redhead's style. It certainly didn't look to Leah as if Ben was suffering any, either. Pam really knew how to turn on the charm when she wanted to. Leah knew that as well as anybody. When Leah had first arrived at the San Francisco Ballet Academy, Pam had been incredibly nice to her and Leah had thought Pam would be one of her closest friends at SFBA. But shortly thereafter, Pam had shown her true colors when she tried to sabotage Leah's audition—and they hadn't really been able to get along since.

"Well, Pam's going to be awfully surprised when Alex gets down here," Leah promised Kay. "Ben seemed to find Alex attractive when she was green and greasy—he'll probably push Pam out of the way to get to Alex when he sees how good she looks now!" Both Kay and Leah giggled.

"What is so funny?" Andrei demanded, slipping between Kay and Leah to get closer to the shrimp bowl. "It is nice to see so much laughing. Everyone has done too much work lately, I think," he added thoughtfully. "Not enough fun. Young persons need to party, no?"

"Yes!" Leah and Kay agreed wholeheartedly.

"Then where is Alex? I hope I did not upset her too much," Andrei said, his grin fading into a mournful look of self-reproach. Leah had noticed that Andrei's moods seemed to change with lightning speed, which probably helped account for the dynamic quality he brought to his dancing. His emotions were quick, strong, and extremely visible.

Leah was about to tell Andrei that Alex would be down in a minute when Alex herself appeared. She paused for a moment, as if sizing up the situation, then, almost like a scene from a fairy-tale ballet, she swept into the room. Her dark hair had a glossy, exotic look to it, and her face glowed a soft pink. She had rolled Michael's jeans up mid-calf, and the white suspenders over the black turtleneck added just the right touch. Alex looked truly sensational.

As if to apologize, Andrei immediately whistled at Alex to tell her that in his opinion she looked great. But it wasn't Andrei's response to Alex that interested Leah—it was Ben Lydgate's. From the look on his face, Pam had ceased to exist the moment Alex returned.

"Uh-oh," Kay said, noticing Ben's reaction to Alex's reappearance. "Pam isn't going to like this."

Leah chuckled. "I know. Isn't it great?"

"Did I miss something?" Andrei asked.

"I think Ben likes Alex," Leah whispered to the Russian dancer.

"*I* like Alex," Andrei said, thumping his chest with his fist.

"Oh, Andrei," Leah groaned, giving him a playful little push. "You know what I mean."

At that moment Ben started walking toward Alex, abandoning Pam for the second time that evening.

"Maybe. But he is not a dancer," Andrei decreed in his thick Russian accent. "Alex will not be interested. I know this."

Once again Ben plucked a rose from the vase on the piano and presented it to Alex, this time with a courtly bow. Alex took the flower and, after breaking off its long stem, fastened the rose to her suspenders.

As Leah continued to watch, awed by the obvious romance of the moment, Alex and Ben began talking. It looked to Leah as if Andrei might be wrong. The pink glow on Alex's face seemed to grow in intensity, and she was practically giggling. Leah had never seen Alex act so—so girlish!

"What do you think they're talking about?" Kay mused. "I mean, they both look so intense."

Before Leah could answer, Pam stormed over, her green eyes flashing. "This certainly isn't my idea of a party," she said, glaring at the trays of food as if they were garbage. "In Atlanta we have *real* parties. I would have had a better time going to sleep early tonight than coming here with *this* crowd."

Andrei chuckled. "We have real parties in Russia also. Lots of drinking, lots of dancing." His eyes seemed to grow wistful for a moment. "But this I like, too. Here," he said, handing Pam a plate on which a tiny eclair swam in a sea of chocolate. "Have a forbidden sweet."

"No thank you," Pam said haughtily. She started to hand back the plate, but instead she bumped the side of Andrei's hand with the plate, causing it to turn sideways. The gooey eclair suddenly slipped off the plate and right down the front of Pam's white satin robe.

"Oh, no! Now look what you've done, you ... you Russian bear!" Pam spat, dropping the plate on the table as the eclair made its way to the floor.

Kenny rushed over to the scene of the disaster. "Look what you guys have done to the Lydgates' Oriental rug! This thing must have cost a fortune."

But Andrei was laughing too hard to apologize, and Pam had gone running out of the room in the same direction Alex had gone earlier that evening.

"Do you think someone ought to go after Pam?" Kay asked Leah.

"Maybe," Leah ventured, "but I'm not going to be the one."

"Where's Ben?" Kenny asked, getting up from the floor where he'd dropped to his hands and knees to pick up the eclair. He put it on a plate and wiped his hands with a napkin. "Maybe Ben knows what we should do to get the chocolate out of the rug."

Leah was about to say "He's right over there." But when she looked over to the spot where Alex and Ben had been talking just a moment earlier, they were gone! She glanced around the room quickly. Neither Alex nor Ben was anywhere in sight.

"It looks like Alex has left with Ben," Kay said.

"It certainly does," Leah commented. "I wonder where they went?"

Chapter 4

Leah had to get up early Sunday morning. The tights she needed for Madame Preston's class needed mending, and she hadn't finished sewing the ribbons on her new toe shoes, either.

Both were tasks Leah had wanted to take care of Saturday night. But by the time Michael had driven her and the other girls home from the party, Leah had been too tired for anything more than a quick shower before collapsing into bed.

The pile of books on her desk reminded Leah that she also had homework to do that day. Among other things, she needed to start on the dance history paper that was due on Friday. She hadn't even settled on a topic yet!

Leah briefly considered skipping Madame Preston's class. That way, she wouldn't have to finish her sewing right away—she could even go back to sleep for a while. After all, the Sunday class was supposedly optional.

The thought of skipping class was so appealing that Leah chucked her satin slippers back in the box beneath her bed and snuggled under her quilt. Leah was just dozing off when there was a gentle knock on her door.

"Leah? It's me." Leah recognized Kay's voice. "Can I come in?"

Leah sighed. It was no use. She threw off her quilt and sat up in bed. "Come on in, Kay."

"You're not up yet?" Kay said, sounding shocked. It was usually Kay who was late getting herself together in the morning, not Leah. "It's after ten," Kay said, indicating Leah's alarm clock with a toss of her head. "Are you sick?"

Leah laughed. "No, just lazy. I was sort of thinking about skipping class this morning." Leah indicated the toe shoes lying in their box beneath her bed. "I still have a ribbon to sew on the left shoe and my old ones are completely shot."

Flinging her dance bag on the floor and reaching for the shoe box, Kay said, "I'll sew while you get dressed."

"You will?" Leah cried. "You're so sweet." Leah grabbed the tights she'd just finished mending and began pulling them on.

"Aren't you going to ask me if I saw Alex this morning?" Kay asked casually.

"That's right! I forgot about Alex and the party. *Have* you seen Alex this morning, Kay?" Leah slipped into her black leotard. Then scooping up her purple sweatshirt from the floor, Leah began turning it right side out.

"No. When I went to the kitchen for a cup of tea, though, Mrs. Hanson told me that Alex had just left," Kay said. She tied a knot in the pink thread, then bit the needle off with her teeth.

"I have scissors, you know," Leah told her with a laugh.

"Teeth are quicker than scissors. We're in a hurry, remember?" Kay reminded Leah. Kay glanced at the clock again, then added, "Oh, my gosh! It's almost ten-thirty. Hurry up, Leah, or there won't be a spot at the barre left for either one of us!"

"I'm all set," Leah said, tossing her brush and a box of hairpins into her dance bag. "How's that ribbon coming?"

Kay held up the toe shoe and smiled. "All done!"

Leah took the shoe from Kay and chucked it into her bag. "All right, then. We're out of here."

As they started down the stairs, Kay said, "Where do you think Alex was going this morning?"

"To class," Leah said. "Where else?"

"It was too early to go to class," Kay insisted.

"Then maybe she was on her way to the library or something. I don't know. What's the big deal?" Leah asked as they reached the first floor.

Kay shrugged. "Nothing, I guess. For some reason, I just thought she might have something interesting to tell us," Kay confessed, a mischievous gleam in her round blue eyes. "Did you ever ask Alex to your house for winter break like you were going to?"

"I didn't get the chance. But I don't think it's winter break that's bothering Alex after all." Leah flexed her foot as the girls paused for a moment in the front hall of the boardinghouse.

"What's bothering her, then? You found out, didn't you?" Kay pressed.

"I think I did, anyway. But you have to promise—"

"Yes, yes," Kay said impatiently. "I promise not to tell anyone—not even Linda, my roommate!"

Leah smiled. "All right, then, I'll tell you. When I went in to help Alex clean up, she blew up at me. She's still really upset about *Temptations*."

"You mean that movie Andrei and James wanted

you to be in with them?" Kay asked, even though Leah was sure Kay knew exactly what *Temptations* was. Kay and the other girls had been nearly as excited as Leah about her having a part in a Hollywood movie.

"Alex wanted the part of Cara Dean, I guess. Although she never came right out and said as much to me, Alex did drop some none-too-subtle hints that I guess I didn't pay much attention to. Remember when a bunch of us were talking about Alex not being invited to join a company yet?"

Kay nodded.

"Well, I guess Alex is pretty upset about that, too. More than she'd ever let on to anybody."

"But Alex did tell you she was upset about that, right?" Kay prompted.

Leah nodded. "Yes, she did. Only I guess I was so wrapped up in whether or not I was going to accept the movie part that I didn't realize how hard it was for Alex to confide in me like that. I feel terrible that I didn't mention her name instead of Diana's to Mr. Rees that day after the *Nutcracker* audition. As Alex pointed out, Diana isn't my friend—Alex is."

"Alex isn't mad now, though, is she?" Kay demanded. "You two are still friends, aren't you?"

Leah shrugged. "I don't know. Alex said we were still friends, but she said that the other day, too, and she was still angry with me."

"Maybe having Ben Lydgate interested in her will make Alex feel better," Kay suggested.

Leah pulled the door of the boardinghouse open. "Don't count on that."

"What do you mean?" Kay asked.

"When we got back from the party last night, I

peeked into Alex's room on my way to the third floor. There she was, sound asleep. It's pretty obvious that Ben Lydgate gave her a ride home almost immediately after she finished getting cleaned up," Leah said. "Alex just didn't want to be at that party, I guess."

"So Andrei was right. Alex could never really be interested in any boy who wasn't a dancer. I know I couldn't. How about you, Leah?" Kay asked.

But there was no time for Leah to answer. The walk light had turned green, and the girls had to hurry across the busy street. Class would be starting in twenty minutes!

"Please wait a moment," Madame Preston said when the applause died down at the end of class. "I have an announcement to make. As some of you may have already heard, the Kirov Ballet will be coming to San Francisco to perform at the War Memorial Opera House."

Instantly the room became engulfed by speculative chatter. Leah took the opportunity to turn around to see Alex's reaction to Madame's news. But it wasn't Alex Leah spotted first—it was Andrei.

Andrei, as everyone knew, had recently defected from the Kirov. Having the company visit San Francisco meant he would be able to see a lot of his old friends. But Andrei was merely staring out the window, looking as if Madame's announcement was of little interest to him.

Alex, on the other hand, was jumping up and down excitedly. Of course, her parents, Olga and Dimitri Sorokin, had danced with the Kirov before their defection, but Alex had been only eleven years old at that time. Then again, Leah thought,

Alex had been a student at the famed Vaganova Institute and some of her fellow students were probably dancing with the Kirov now. After all, Alex was nearly eighteen years old. Leah had to smile. It was good to see Alex so happy.

"Quiet," Madame said, raising her arms. "Quiet, please." Once order had been restored to the studio, Madame continued.

"Unfortunately, all of my news is not good. First of all, the Kirov will be giving only four performances, partially due to their schedule and partially due to our own *Nutcracker* schedule.

"Secondly, there will be no complimentary tickets to their performances. And tickets, I'm afraid, are going to be both scarce and expensive. Still, I hope everyone in this room will make the effort to see at least one performance. In fact, we are canceling our own Friday night *Nutcracker* rehearsals so that you may use that time to attend. I believe they will be dancing *Swan Lake* that evening, but I may be wrong. Anyway, they will not be dancing *The Nutcracker*, for which we should all be thankful!" A few students giggled at Madame's joke, and she paused to smile, too.

"Last of all," Madame said, the smile disappearing from her stern face, "and I'm afraid this is the hardest news of all for me to pass along, Alexandra Sorokin and Andrei Levintoff are to stay away from the Opera House while the Kirov is here, for security reasons. That means both during rehearsals *and* during performances. I'm sorry, but both the Soviet and the U.S. authorities believe this to be in the best interests of all concerned."

So Alex wasn't going to be able to see the Kirov after all! Leah said to herself. And Alex had been so excited, too—more excited than Leah had seen her act in a long time. Suddenly Leah remembered what Alex had said to her the other night. Alex had said that the ballet world sometimes made her feel like a bird in a cage. Madame, it seemed, had just padlocked Alex's cage door. Leah felt deeply concerned for her friend, who looked upset by the news.

However, Andrei seemed completely unfazed by the unpleasant twist in Madame's exciting news. He was still looking out the window as if nothing that had been said had anything to do with him. But then, Leah had learned that it was very difficult to read Andrei's emotions.

"One more thing. I must ask all of you to notify me immediately of any suspicious-looking people loitering about the school, or Mrs. Hanson's boardinghouse," Madame said. "Precautions have been taken, but I feel we must be alert."

Then her scowl lifted as she said, "So, let's all make the most of this visit and the opportunity it presents us." With that, Madame turned and swept gracefully out of the studio.

As Leah started toward the dressing room, Kay caught up with her.

"What do you think, Leah?" she whispered, grabbing Leah's arm. "Doesn't this sound like something right out of a James Bond story? Spies, foreign intrigue, and everything else!"

"Shh!" Leah told her. "I think Alex is really upset about not being allowed to see the Kirov dance. We've got to be careful not to make her any more upset."

Kay nodded. "Of course! You're right, Leah."

When Kay and Leah entered the dressing room,

Alex was brushing out her luxurious black hair in front of the mirror, next to Pam.

"Too bad, Sorokin," Pam said, without a hint of sympathy in her voice, as she braided her auburn hair.

"Yes," Alex agreed sadly. "It is more than too bad. To be denied the opportunity to see ballet danced by *real* ballet dancers is a tragedy."

"Are you saying that the Bay Area Ballet isn't a real—" Pam began, but Kay didn't let her finish.

"And it really doesn't make a lot of sense, either," Kay contended angrily, despite the warning that Leah had just given her. "I mean, I can understand why Andrei might be a risk. The Soviets might just try to force him to go back with them. But why you? You're just a student. Besides, Andrei recently defected, and you defected years ago. I mean, you were a child!"

Alex nodded as she tossed her brush into her dance bag. "You are absolutely right, Kay. Why would the renowned Kirov Ballet even know of my existence, much less want to do anything about it?" By now Alex sounded more angry than sad; it almost sounded as if she *wished* the Kirov would try to force her back to Russia.

"I have a good idea," Leah said cheerfully, hoping to put an end to the unpleasant discussion. "Let's do something fun this afternoon."

"I'd planned to go to the Asian Art Museum in Golden Gate Park this afternoon," Kay announced. "They're holding a Kabuki lecture and staging a performance there that I'm really excited about. Why don't you and Alex come with me?"

Leah nodded thoughtfully. "You know, I still don't have a topic for my dance history paper.

Maybe I'll get an idea at the museum. How about it, Alex? Want to come?"

Alex shook her head. "No, I have things I must do."

"We'll be back before six o'clock," Kay promised.

"I have things that must be done before six," Alex said quickly, not offering any more of an explanation. Then, flinging her dance bag over her shoulder, the Russian girl said her good-byes and left.

Had Alex been blushing as she slipped through the door, Leah wondered. Or had she merely been flushed with the indignation of being excluded from the Kirov performances? Leah glanced over at Kay.

"I guess Alex wants to be alone," Kay offered.

"I guess so," Leah agreed. Stepping up to the spot at the mirror that Alex had just vacated, Leah began letting down her hair.

Meanwhile, Pam had finished braiding her thick red hair. She turned to face Leah and Kay. "Why don't you two quit trying to mother everyone around here and mind your own business for a change? Alex is a big girl, you know. She can take care of herself."

"Thanks, Pam," Kay said sarcastically. "Your compassionate words of concern for your fellow students are always welcome."

"Madame Preston herself asked all of us to look out for Alex," Leah reminded Pam. "You must have heard her say to watch for any suspicious-looking characters lurking about. Alex might be in danger, you know."

"Well, Andrei certainly didn't seem very worried, and as Kay herself pointed out, if the Soviets are interested in anyone around here, it's Andrei and not Alex," Pam retorted. "I personally think Madame is being overly dramatic. Performers often are, you know." And with that Pam stormed out of the dressing room, acting every bit as dramatic as she was accusing the Academy's director of being.

Chapter 5

Leah pulled the collar of her dark blue wool coat up around her neck. For once, it wasn't raining. But the sky was overcast, and it looked as if it might start pouring any second. The damp and cold made Leah long for her hometown of San Lorenzo. She was certain that at that very moment, the sun was beating down on the artichoke farms of the little inland valley town.

"When is the bus supposed to come?" Leah asked, turning anxiously to Kay.

"Any minute, according to the schedule," Kay assured her, leaning out and peering down the street.

"Today's bus schedule? It's Sunday, you know," Leah reminded her friend, who could be scatter-brained at times. "The buses run differently on Sundays than they do the rest of the week."

"Yes," Kay said patiently, "I know. It was Sunday's schedule that I checked. I've been looking forward to this Kabuki thing for a couple of weeks. I'll kill myself if I miss it because of a dumb bus."

Leah turned her legs out from the hips, her heels touching and her feet almost forming a

46

straight line. Then, Leah began to hum Tchaikov-sky's *Nutcracker*.

"What are you doing?" Kay asked, eyeing Leah with amusement.

"Pretending I'm not here." Leah dropped her arms to her side with a sigh. "Actually, I shouldn't be here. I said I'd go with you so that Alex would come, too. I thought if she did something with us, it would cheer her up."

"Thanks a lot!" Kay snorted. "What's wrong with my company?"

"Nothing," Leah said quickly. "What I mean is, I have a lot to do. I have laundry and mending and that dance history paper, not to mention other homework."

"But I think this Kabuki performance will really help you think of a topic for your paper, just like you said." Kay's voice sounded almost pleading, and Leah realized she was going to have to go with Kay or risk hurting her feelings.

Leah sighed. Everyone seemed so sensitive lately! Maybe it was the holidays, after all. Or maybe it was the strain of preparing for their first full-length ballet with the Bay Area Ballet Company.

"You're probably right," Leah conceded. "Any-way, here comes the bus."

"You know, Leah," Kay said after they got on the bus and took their seats, "the more I think about this whole thing with Alex and Andrei and the Kirov Ballet, the more I don't understand what the big deal is! I guess I can understand why Andrei shouldn't try to socialize with his old friends. I can see why the Soviets wouldn't want that."

Leah chuckled. "Do you think Andrei might try to get his friends at the Kirov to defect, too?"

Kay shrugged. "If I was involved with the Kirov, I might think about it. But it seems a little silly to keep both of them from attending a performance. What could happen during a performance? There's security all over the place. None of the dancers could escape. And what do *our* authorities have to worry about? That one really has me confused."

Leah slowly flexed her right foot, trying to feel each of the muscles separately, the way Madame had taught them in class that morning. "Maybe there's more to all this than there seems to be," she told Kay as she repeated the flexing motion with her left foot.

"At first I was just thinking how unfair it was to keep Alex from seeing the Kirov," Leah went on. "But I don't know anymore. I have this weird feeling that something could happen to either Alex or Andrei if they aren't careful."

"You mean kidnapping?" Kay demanded.

Leah nodded. "It doesn't seem too surprising to me that the Soviets might want Andrei back again. I mean, from their perspective he's probably a fugitive or something."

"But what about Alex?" Kay mused. "What could the Soviets want from her? They wouldn't want her to dance for them, would they?"

"Why not? Alex is good, one of the best," Leah retorted, defending her Russian friend.

"I didn't mean it like that," Kay insisted.

"Well, you should be careful. I think you might have hurt Alex's feelings back there in the dressing room." Leah tucked an errant wisp of blond hair behind her ear.

Kay looked genuinely shocked. "You're right! How dumb of me! I only meant that Alex hasn't gotten all of her training at the Vaganova Institute the way Andrei has. He was already a soloist for the Kirov when he defected. The Russians are very fussy about training—it's incredibly thorough, and probably pretty expensive, too. Each of their dancers is like a government investment." Kay paused. Then suddenly her blue eyes lit up. "I've got it! I know why Alex is in danger!" she said excitedly.

"Tell me," Leah ordered.

"It's her *parents*. I bet the Kirov wants the Sorokins back. If the KGB were to kidnap Alex—"

"Come on, Kay. Don't be ridiculous," Leah told her. "I don't think our government would allow such a thing."

"Exactly," Kay said. "The Soviets will be trying to kidnap Alex and Andrei, and our government will be trying to stop them! Doesn't it seem obvious that that's what's going on?"

Briefly, Leah considered Kay's idea. "I don't know. Kidnapping a girl to blackmail her parents wouldn't make the Soviets look very good to the rest of the world."

"Shhh, someone might be following us at this very moment!" Kay whispered as she glanced nervously from side to side.

Leah laughed in spite of herself. "Why would anyone follow *us*, Kay? Are they going to kidnap us, too?"

"Go ahead," Kay said, turning slightly in her seat to look over her shoulder. "Laugh. But we're Alex's best friends. If they're after her, it would make sense for them to keep an eye on us. They might want to figure out our daily schedules or something like that."

Leah was about to protest Kay's theory again when the diminutive dancer grabbed Leah's arm so hard that Leah gasped in pain. "Don't look now, Leah, but there's a suspicious-looking couple sitting at the back of this bus. I'm sure they're watching us, too."

"That doesn't surprise me. This bus isn't very crowded, and you've been talking kind of loudly, Kay," Leah pointed out.

"Shhh!" Kay held her finger to her lips. "Don't say another word about any of this. I'm sure those people are spies."

"Then it's a good thing our stop is next. Come on." Leah got to her feet. As soon as Kay had stepped into the aisle in front of Leah, Leah took Kay by the elbow and whisked her toward the front of the bus. "When we get off at the next corner, I guarantee we'll never see those people again."

"Leah," Kay whispered urgently as the bus continued down the street toward the museum. "Don't look, but that couple is *still* watching us!"

Glancing behind her, Leah saw that there was indeed a couple in the back, and they seemed to be staring right back at her. It was hard to tell for sure, though, because they were both wearing sunglasses.

Sunglasses! Who, Leah asked herself, would wear *sunglasses* on a cloudy day? And not only were they sporting dark shades, they were also wearing matching trench coats and brown felt hats with low brims. In fact, they looked just like the spies Leah had seen on television.

Suddenly, the bus lurched to a stop, and the front door swung open. The couple stood up and quickly made their way down the aisle to the bus's rear door. They were getting off the bus at the same stop as Leah and Kay!

An uneasy feeling swept over Leah as she descended the steps of the bus to the curb. *Remain calm,* Leah ordered herself. Kay, she knew from experience, could be a virtual hysteric. So it was up to Leah to maintain their sanity and get them out of a potentially dangerous situation.

"Come on, Kay," Leah said, taking charge. "We better hurry, or we won't get good seats for the show." Leah planned to hurry Kay into the Asian Art Museum, where they would quickly lose the strange-looking couple in the crowd. Hopefully, Kay wouldn't even notice that they were being followed.

Leah picked up the pace and Kay matched her long-legged stride, but the couple was still right behind them. Leah made a mental note to tell Madame Preston about the suspicious pair as soon as she got back to their boardinghouse.

"Why are we walking so fast? We're not late," Kay observed, eyeing Leah curiously. Then she glanced over her shoulder and gasped. The couple had picked up the pace, and they were now gaining on the two girls. "Oh, no!" Kay cried. Closing her eyes and hunching her shoulders forward, she came to a complete stop.

Leah felt herself panic as the forceful footsteps of the mysterious couple drew closer and closer. Leah wasn't at all certain what they wanted, but there was no doubt in Leah's mind now that this couple wanted something!

Suddenly, the footsteps overtook them ... but they didn't stop. The couple strode on past the girls, on up the walkway, and into the museum.

"Kay," Leah said, gently shaking her friend. "It's okay. They're gone."

Kay slowly opened her eyes. "Where did they go?" she asked so softly Leah was barely able to hear.

"Into the museum," Leah replied.

"Come on." Kay turned around. "Let's catch the next bus back to Mrs. Hanson's. We've got to report those people!"

"What can we report?" Leah asked. "All they really did was look at us and then get off at our stop."

"But they were wearing those sunglasses, and they went into the museum!" Kay cried excitedly.

Leah shook her head. "Going into the museum isn't a crime, and neither is wearing sunglasses. Those people were dressed strangely, but that was about all they were guilty of."

"I still think we ought to go home," Kay said. "I don't think it's safe here."

"And miss the Kabuki dancers? I really want to see them," Leah insisted. "I know you do, too."

"Our safety is more important than the show," Kay retorted.

"I don't think anyone is going to do anything to *us*, Kay. Let's suppose, for a moment, that those people *were* Russian spies. The only reason I can come up with for them following us is that they thought Alex was going to be with us." Leah shrugged. "She isn't, so they quit following us."

"Maybe they think she's going to meet us here," Kay suggested.

"Or maybe we were both just imagining things," Leah pointed out. "Either way, getting all excited isn't going to do Alex or Andrei or us any good. I think we ought to just go about our business. Then, if those two *are* spies, we'll be doing Alex a favor by keeping them occupied all afternoon. And if they aren't, then everything's okay. Right?"

"But shouldn't we call Madame?" Kay asked. "Or maybe we should warn Alex."

Leah shook her head. "I think it's too soon to call Madame. Granted, she did say we should tell her about any suspicious-looking people—but only the ones we saw hanging around school or the boardinghouse. Madame didn't say anything about weird people on buses. There are a lot of characters in San Francisco, you know."

"But what about Alex?" Kay pressed.

"No," Leah said thoughtfully. "There's no point in worrying Alex if there's nothing to worry about. She's been edgy enough lately as it is."

Kay shrugged. "All right, then. We'll wait." With that, the girls continued up the walk to the museum.

As they slowly entered the domed foyer, both Leah and Kay searched the crowd milling around the entrance to the gift shop. Then they checked the crowd sitting along the curved walls of the foyer on white marble benches. But the couple from the bus was nowhere to be found.

"They've disappeared," Leah said, feeling immensely relieved.

"Maybe they're inside the museum somewhere," Kay suggested. "Or maybe they're in the rest room."

"Which one?" Leah asked, unable to stop herself from smiling. "If it's the men's, you'll have to check it out yourself, Kay."

"Go ahead and laugh," Kay said indignantly. "I don't think this is very funny."

"I'm sorry," Leah apologized. "I don't really think it's funny either, and yet ..." She started laughing again and this time Kay joined her.

"I'm so nervous," Kay confessed once their laughter was under control.

"You and me both," Leah confirmed. "Let's buy our tickets and go in. Maybe the show will take our minds off things."

"Let's just hope those two aren't waiting outside the museum to jump us when we come out," Kay muttered.

"Kay!" Leah cried. "Cut it out."

"I'm sorry. I was only kidding. It was a bad joke, wasn't it?"

But Kay's idea of someone lurking outside waiting to grab them wasn't easy for Leah to dismiss. After all, by six o'clock that evening it would be dark!

As they waited for the elevator to take them to the second floor theater, Leah considered calling the police. She wanted to ask Kay what she thought, but Kay looked as if she had already put the incident out of her mind. Kay was like that, Leah reflected: easily upset, easily distracted. Not wanting to alarm her again, Leah decided she'd come up with a plan herself and simply tell Kay about it later.

At the entrance to the small museum theater, they were each handed a program. Then Leah and Kay started down the aisle to find seats. Suddenly, Kay let out a startled gasp.

"What's wrong?" Leah asked nervously.

Kay lifted her slender arm and pointed to the stage. There, right in front of the girls, was the couple from the bus! They had taken off their dark glasses and shed their trench coats and fedoras. Now, smiling and sitting at a long table on the stage, they appeared to be a perfectly nice, middle-aged Japanese couple.

Not knowing what else to do, Leah slid into the nearest seat, certain that her face had turned a deep shade of red. "I don't know about you, Kay, but I feel like an idiot," Leah whispered. She hoped with all her heart that the Japanese couple didn't know what the girls had been thinking about them.

"Maybe we were wrong *this* time," Kay conceded as she sat down next to Leah. She didn't seem the least bit embarrassed by their mistake. "But that hardly means that Alex and Andrei aren't in some kind of danger."

"I don't know about that," Leah mused. "As far as I can tell, the biggest danger Alex is facing at the moment is missing the Kirov dance."

Kay looked as if she were going to say something more. But before she could, the lights dimmed and the man they had thought was a spy began chronicling the development of Kabuki dance in Japan while slides flashed on a wide screen beside him.

For the moment, at least, Leah forgot about Alex, spies, and the Kirov Ballet.

Chapter 6

Leah had just finished the last of her geometry homework when there was a knock on her bedroom door. "It's us," Kay announced. "Can we come in?"

"That depends. Who exactly is 'us'?" Leah called back.

Kay opened the door and stuck her head in. "It's me and *Alex,*" Kay said. "We thought we'd bring our sewing up here on the outside chance that you would be doing yours."

"Come on in!" Leah exclaimed, glad that Kay had managed to coax Alex out of her room. "That's *exactly* what I was about to do."

"Hello, Leah," Alex said, following Kay into Leah's cozy third floor room. After shooing Misha off Leah's bed, Alex set down a tea tray where the little orange cat had been sitting. "Kay and I decided this chilly night called for some hot tea."

"And a couple of Mrs. Hanson's 'diet' cookies," Kay added as she tossed an armful of tights and a sewing basket onto Leah's bed. After letting out a loud meow, Misha jumped back up on the bed and settled himself comfortably in the pile of tights.

Leah sat up and gathered her cat into her arms

as she swung her feet over the edge of the bed. "This sounds better all the time, doesn't it, Misha?"

Misha meowed again. Then, freeing himself from Leah's grasp, he jumped nimbly to the floor and sashayed out the bedroom door.

"Shall I get him?" Kay asked.

Leah shook her head. "No, let him go. He likes to visit people."

"You mean Pam, don't you?" Kay said.

Leah shrugged. She would never understand why her cat preferred Pam's company, but as long as Pam was nice to Misha, she didn't really mind.

While Kay and Leah had been discussing Misha, Alex had poured three steaming cups of tea. "Milk?" she asked. When both Leah and Kay nodded, Alex added a touch of milk from a small porcelain pitcher to their cups.

Alex handed Kay and Leah their tea. Then, with her own cup in hand, Alex sat down on the floor next to Kay. "So," she said, "tell me what you think of the Kabuki. Kay tells me I missed much excitement. She would not reveal any details, though. Kay says I must wait for you to do that."

Leah and Kay exchanged glances.

"It was a wonderful presentation," Leah answered after taking a sip of tea. "I don't know if it will help me with my dance history paper, but it was well worth seeing."

"It *was* good," Kay agreed enthusiastically. "But the real excitement happened before the presentation. Right, Leah?" Kay winked.

Leah shook her head. She couldn't believe that Kay actually wanted to tell Alex about the spies who weren't spies. Just thinking about that whole episode embarrassed Leah all over again. "I'm not sure we should go into all that right now, Kay."

"Go into what?" Alex asked, her dark eyebrows drawn together in a scowl. Remembering how hurt Alex had been when she'd felt left out of the plans for *Temptations,* Leah decided Alex should know the whole story—what there was of it. When Leah really thought about it, their "close call" was funnier than it was anything else. Alex could probably use a good laugh at this point.

"Oh, all right," Leah relented. "Go ahead and tell Alex about our exciting episode, Kay. I suppose she already knows how silly we are anyway."

Kay let out a tiny giggle and proceeded to tell Alex about the spies who turned out to be the chief lecturers at the Asian Art Museum. By the time she reached the end of the story, Alex was laughing so hard that tears were streaming down her face.

"You both are too much," Alex told them, tears spilling from her cheeks to the pillow she'd been clutching against her stomach. "Like the blind following each other."

Kay and Leah looked at each other and started laughing all over again.

"Did I say something funny?" Alex demanded, taking a tissue from the box on the table beside Leah's bed to dry her eyes.

"You got the idea right," Kay told her, "but the way that expression really goes is, 'Like the blind *leading* the blind.' And you're absolutely right about that. We got each other so scared that we were ready to call the police. Right, Leah?"

Leah nodded. "I know I was. When they turned

out to be lecturers on the panel, I was so glad we hadn't done anything. Imagine if the police had arrested them in the middle of the slide show! It would have been mortifying."

"But, you know," Kay said thoughtfully, "this whole experience made me realize something. Madame Preston has probably blown this Kirov thing way out of proportion, too—just like we did. I'm sure there's some tension, particularly between Andrei and the officials at the Kirov. But to think that anyone is in danger ..." Kay let her voice trail off as she finished her thought with a dubious shrug of her shoulders.

Leah nodded. "I think you're right, Kay. Maybe we should talk to Madame and see if she'll change her mind about letting Alex go to Friday's performance with us." Then, remembering Alex's admonition to stop trying to plan her life for her, Leah added, "What do you think, Alex? I bet we could change Madame's mind. I'm even willing to tell her how foolish Kay and I acted this afternoon."

"I do not think it wise," Alex said with a shrug. "Madame said I was not to see the Kirov dance. I am sad, but this is what must be."

Alex's reaction surprised Leah. That very morning Alex had seemed devastated about not being allowed to attend a performance of the famous Russian company. Now she was acting as if she couldn't care less.

But then, Alex had been acting peculiar in many ways lately. In some ways, Leah felt as if she didn't understand Alex at all anymore. However, if Alex had decided to accept the fact that certain authorities didn't want her to see the Kirov, Leah wasn't about to argue with her.

Leah got out her sewing basket and a few pairs of tights that needed mending. She was trying to think of a way to change the subject when Kay exclaimed as she threw down her sewing, "But missing the Kirov dance seems so unfair! If I were you, I'd be furious, Alex. What am I saying? I'm *not* you, Alex, and I'm still furious. The government, any government really, just doesn't understand the needs of artists. You shouldn't put up with this."

With a half smile playing at her lips, Alex said, "Sometimes it is better not to challenge authority."

Unable to keep silent any longer, Leah said, "Alex, I can't believe you aren't still upset, either. I mean, you were *so* down about it this morning after class. And now, well, it seems like the Kirov means nothing to you."

Alex's pale cheeks seemed to flush slightly as she bent more intently over the stitches she was taking to repair her pink tights. "I was upset this morning. But what is the use of being upset over something I cannot change? As unfair as Madame's decision seems, it is her decision. I must accept it. If I do not, I will simply suffer, for nothing. She will not change her mind. I know that."

"I think I know why this isn't bothering you," Kay said, setting down one pair of tights and picking up another. Then, looking up again, Kay smiled. "I think you have a secret plan."

Alex looked up sharply. "What do you mean by secret plan, Kay Larkin?"

Startled by Alex's sudden vehemence, Leah said, "Why are you so jumpy, Alex? I mean, one minute you tell us that you're no longer upset. Then the next minute you bristle when Kay teases you a little bit. This isn't like you at all!"

Alex looked sheepish. "Of course, you are right, Leah. I guess I am a little upset still. The Kirov, you know, is like extended family to me. When Madame said they come to San Francisco, I think for a brief moment I would have a chance to unlock the secret of my own dancing. But now I am resigned to my fate. The Kirov Ballet is forbidden to me. The secret, if there even is one, must remain locked away."

"I think you're giving up too easily," Kay proclaimed. "If someone told me I wasn't allowed to see Lynne Vreeland, my own mother, dance, I know what I'd do."

Leah nodded, remembering what Kay *had* done when her famous mother, Lynne Vreeland, had come to San Francisco to dance. For the most part, Kay had hidden out, trying to avoid her mother. But Leah certainly didn't want to bring that unhappy time up now. Instead, she said, "Tell us what you'd do, Kay."

"Remember in *The Nutcracker* where I come out in a stiff little peasant girl costume and pretend to be one of Drosselmeyer's clockwork toys?" Kay asked.

"Come on, Kay, get to the point," Leah urged.

"Alex can do the same thing!" Kay said, throwing her hands up in the air and smiling as if she'd just said something terribly profound. But before either Leah or Alex could ask Kay to explain exactly what she was driving at, the buzzer that signaled a phone call for one of the girls began to sound.

"Three short buzzes!" Alex cried, leaping to her

feet. "It is a call for me!" Carelessly tossing her tights on top of her half-full cup of tea, Alex turned and bolted from Leah's room.

"I wonder ..." But before Leah could finish saying that she wondered who was calling Alex at this time on a Sunday night, Kay was also on her feet. She dashed out the door after Alex.

Shaking her head at the hasty exit of both her friends, Leah got to her feet and pulled Alex's tights from her teacup. Just as Leah had feared, the pink tights were stained with tea. Grabbing a few sheets of Kleenex from the dispenser on her bedside table, Leah tried her best to blot them dry.

Leah was still working on soaking up the stain when Kay returned, carrying the blond wig she was supposed to wear as Clara in *The Nutcracker.* Leah knew that Kay loathed the wig, and she could hardly blame her.

"I just knew this dumb thing would come in handy sometime," Kay said. She was holding the wig out in front of her as if it were a dead animal instead of an integral part of her costume.

"Now what?" Leah wondered aloud.

"This is the answer to Alex's problem," Kay announced triumphantly.

"What problem?" Alex inquired as she practically floated into the room with a wide grin on her face.

With great ceremony Kay handed the wig to Alex. "The wig is your ticket to the Kirov Ballet."

Alex looked confused. "But I do not need ticket. I am not going to ballet."

"Oh yes you are. We're going to put together a disguise for you, Alex. If no one recognizes you, there shouldn't be any problem with you being there, right?" Kay asked.

Leah smiled. "You know, Alex, Kay might be right. You know what they always say, don't you? 'Nothing ventured, nothing gained.'"

" 'Nothing ventured, nothing gained,'" Alex repeated thoughtfully. Then she smiled. "I like that one. I will remember it. 'Nothing ventured, nothing gained,'" Alex said again slowly.

"This *is* going to work," Kay insisted. "I just know it is. Put the wig on, Alex."

Alex, still grinning, slipped on the wig. "It feels awful!" Alex complained, sliding it first forward and then backward on her head.

Kay nodded solemnly. "Try to imagine dancing in it like I have to! But it does change your looks an awful lot. Doesn't it, Leah?"

"But not enough," Leah pointed out. "You just look like Alex in a wig. We've got to get you out of those black clothes of yours." Leah turned to her dresser and pulled open the middle drawer. "What about these?" she asked, holding up her favorite pair of purple overalls.

Alex shook her head. "Absolutely not," she said firmly. "I will not go to the Opera House in overalls."

"Alex has a point," Kay agreed. "She needs to blend into the crowd, not stand out. What she needs is a smashing dress and—" Kay paused, and her round blue eyes surveyed Leah's room. "And that!" Kay declared, pointing at Leah's flowered rain hat.

"*That?*" Alex didn't sound convinced. The plastic hat was a bright shade of green, definitely not

Alex's style—and not very easily hid in the crowd, either.

"Well, something like that. A hat would make that wig look a little more natural," Kay said authoritatively.

Alex didn't look exactly thrilled with Kay's idea, Leah noted. But then again, she hadn't stormed out of the room yet, either. She merely looked thoughtful.

"So? What do you think, Alex?" Leah asked cautiously. "Do you want to try to slip into the Opera House incognito?"

"All right," Alex finally said, a hint of mischief in her eyes. "I will try what you suggest." She walked to Leah's closet and picked out a long-sleeved knit dress of Leah's in a soft violet color. "May I borrow this?" she asked, holding the dress up against her body.

"Of course," Leah said. Kay looked triumphantly at Leah, and Leah couldn't help but return her friend's infectious grin. It felt good to be doing something to cheer up Alex. In fact, Leah felt as if her wavering friendship with Alex was once again on solid ground.

"Great!" Kay exclaimed, taking back her wig. "I'd like to give you this right now, but unfortunately I need it for rehearsals. I'll have to slip it to you Friday afternoon. Meanwhile, I'll get tickets for the three of us tomorrow."

Just then Mrs. Hanson popped her head into Leah's room. "It's awfully late, girls, and you're being kind of loud up here, you know."

"Oh, my gosh!" Leah exclaimed, startled. She looked at the clock. "It *is* late."

"Abigail just came downstairs to my room to

complain that you were keeping her awake," Mrs. Hanson said firmly. Then, a little more kindly, she added, "Hand me those tea things, will you, Kay dear? I'll run them down to the kitchen for you girls." Kay passed the tray to her. Then the girls thanked Mrs. Hanson and said good night.

After Mrs. Hanson was gone, Leah said quietly, "I hope Abby didn't hear what we were talking about."

"Abigail would have said something to Mrs. Hanson if she had heard us. She is too much of a tattletale to keep something like this secret," Alex reasoned.

Leah nodded. "I think you're right, Alex. But from now on, we've got to be careful or we'll all get into trouble." Leah handed Alex her tights. "You dropped these in your tea when you went to get the phone."

"Thanks," Alex said, taking the tights from Leah and examining the stain nonchalantly. "I have something that should get this mark out."

"Who was on the phone, anyway?" Leah asked, trying to sound casual.

"I will tell you about it another time," Alex said, dramatically stifling a yawn. "Come on, Kay. I must get to bed before I fall asleep on my feet."

"Me, too," Kay agreed. "Well, good night Leah," she said as they tiptoed out the door.

"Good night," Leah whispered back.

Once she was alone, Leah slipped off her terry-cloth robe and hung it neatly in her closet. Carefully, Leah transferred her geometry book and notebook to her desk and tucked her sewing basket back beneath her bed. Then she put her soft pink dancing shoes into her dance bag. Taking one last look around, Leah felt satisfied that everything was in its place.

After running a brush through her hair one last time, Leah climbed wearily into bed, certain she would be asleep the instant her head hit the pillow. But as soon as she turned out the lights, she felt wide awake. There was so much on her mind that she felt she had to figure out.

Who, Leah wondered, had called Alex so late at night? It was someone who'd made Alex happy; that much was obvious by the smile on Alex's face and the slight flush that had colored her usually pale cheeks. But why had Alex been so secretive about the call if it had been good news?

Then all at once Leah sat bolt upright in bed. Alexandra's parents were probably coming to San Francisco! And why not? The holidays were right around the corner, and the Kirov Ballet was going to be in town.

But what about the Soviet authorities, Leah asked herself? What would they do if they found out the Sorokins were around? What if the KGB decided to forget kidnapping Alex and go after the older Sorokins? Perhaps the whole family would be taken back to the Soviet Union!

Then Leah remembered that she and Kay had only been guessing about the KGB wanting to kidnap Alex in the first place—it wasn't real. Leah knew she was just being silly again. She was so tired that she was imagining things, getting herself worked up about nothing—just as she had earlier that day.

Leah had almost drifted off to sleep when she heard the faint sound of the telephone ringing on the first floor. It was five after one in the morning, according to her clock. Leah flicked on the light. Then, after slipping on her robe, she started downstairs to see if it had been the telephone, or if she was starting to go crazy.

Leah was about halfway down the second flight of stairs when she heard Alex's low, throaty laugh coming from the downstairs hall. Peering over the railing, Leah saw Alex sitting on the floor in the dark hall. She was still dressed in her black jeans and her black crepe blouse, and she was on the telephone ... again!

Leah was still staring at her friend in disbelief when Alex suddenly looked up in Leah's direction. Alex leapt to her feet, her face registering pure panic. The haunted look in her Russian friend's almond-shaped eyes made Leah feel like *she'd* been caught spying. Clearly, Alex hadn't wanted to be overheard by anyone, not even Leah.

Leah felt like turning around and running back to her room, but she couldn't pretend that nothing had happened. Running away, Leah knew, would only add to the awkwardness of the situation and probably make Alex even madder. It would make Leah look guilty, when she hadn't heard anything at all. Alex had to know that Leah hadn't been sneaking around, eavesdropping on her. That was typical Pamela Hunter behavior— not at all Leah's style.

"Are you okay?" Leah asked in a loud whisper so that Alex would understand her intentions. "Is everything all right with your parents?"

Alex looked confused. "My parents?" she asked. Then her look of panic melted into a relieved smile. Covering the mouthpiece of the phone with her hand, Alex said, "My parents are fine. I am fine. We are all hunky-dory." Then Alex waved Leah back up the stairs with her hand. "Go to bed," she mouthed.

Leah still wanted to know what was going on, but she knew that Alex wasn't going to share whatever it was, at least not at the moment. Leah would simply have to be patient and trust her friend. Alex would fill Leah in ... if and when she wanted to.

Chapter 7

The sun was shining brightly as Leah stepped out of Mrs. Hanson's boardinghouse, and it seemed more like summer to her than mid-December. There wasn't even any wind, and the dampness in the air had vanished. Leah closed her eyes and held her face skyward to soak up the glorious rays.

Suddenly, a chilly wind came up out of no-where. Opening her eyes, Leah saw that the sky had blackened. A wet blanket of fog was drifting rapidly toward her from the bay. Leah held her hands to her cheeks and took a couple of steps backward. Then, looking down, Leah discovered she wasn't dressed in street clothes as she had thought. Instead, she was wearing the pink tights and black leotard that were regulation student dress at SFBA. She wasn't wearing a coat and, strangest of all, she was wearing her pink satin pointe shoes!

Leah was about to return to the boardinghouse to change when she heard a scuffling noise behind her. Nervously she began to turn around, but suddenly she found herself on pointe, preparing for a series of fouettés.

"Leah!" a desperate voice called just as Leah

finished her last turn. Leah looked around, but the street in front of Mrs. Hanson's appeared to be deserted.

"Leah!" the voice called again, and Leah recognized a familiar Russian accent. It was Alex! She was directly across the street, and two men in trench coats and wide-brimmed felt hats were dragging her away!

"Leah!" Alex yelled in an anguished voice. "You must help me! You must stop them!"

Leah wanted to help her friend, but she could not. Leah was dancing a solo, and she couldn't make herself stop!

All of a sudden Alex broke free and started dancing a pas de trois with the two men in trench coats. Leah wondered if Alex really wanted to be saved, or if her calls weren't simply part of her dance. She strained to see who Alex's partners were, hoping that the identity of the men would shed some light on what was really happening. Was Alex in danger, or was this simply theater, Leah asked herself. But both men were wearing sunglasses, and Leah couldn't tell what was going on.

Springing straight into the air as Leah watched, Alex performed a brilliant series of entrechats, crisp and daring. The men paused in their pursuit, but only briefly. While one man continued to hold back, the other closed in on Alex. Taking hold of her waist, he supported Alex through a series of pirouettes. Then he held her high above his head in a swallow lift.

"Farewell, my friend," Alex remarked as the first man carried her away with the second man trailing behind them. But Leah was still dancing her solo and could not speak, could not even stop to say good-bye to her best friend. Speaking even one word, Leah knew, would break her concentration and ruin her dance.

As Leah prepared for a grand jeté, she felt hot tears of anguish and regret spill down her cheeks. Leah knew that she was never going to see her friend again. Alex's farewell had been final.

Suddenly, a loud buzzer went off in the distance. Leah tried to escape the frightening noise by gliding away from its source with a series of sharp bourrées. But the harder she worked, the louder the buzzer became, until finally Leah thought the evil noise must be inside her own head!

"Leah!" a voice shouted above the sound. Leah forced herself to open her eyes even though the buzzing sound continued. "Leah, wake up!"

"Kay?" Leah asked, recognizing her petite friend. As soon as she'd spoken Kay's name, Leah realized she was in bed and in her own room. She'd been dreaming! But somehow, knowing that didn't make Leah feel much better. The dream had been so real! The danger had seemed so pressing. Poor Alexandra!

"What's wrong?" Kay asked, her smile changing into a look of concern. "You aren't sick, are you?"

Leah sat up. "Oh, Kay!" she cried. "I had the most awful dream!"

Kay turned off Leah's alarm. "You better start worrying about reality instead of your dream. Class starts in twenty minutes, and you know how angry Mr. Robson gets if we're late."

"Oh, no," Leah wailed at the thought of Christopher Robson, a renowned danseur who had once partnered Leah's former teacher back in San Lorenzo, Hannah Greene. Mr. Robson was now a guest instructor at SFBA, and his stern style had been the source of more than one headache for Leah. "It is his day to teach our morning class, isn't it?"

Kay nodded as she handed Leah her pink tights. "And we're going to be rehearsing with him this afternoon, too. Don't forget he's Drosselmeyer in *The Nutcracker*."

Leah couldn't help laughing. "Now, *that* was a brilliant piece of casting!" she exclaimed. Now that she was awake and Kay was with her, Leah's dream didn't seem as awful as it had only moments earlier.

Leah quickly dressed, then began detangling her long blond hair. "Rats!" Leah cried in exasperation as she struggled with a particularly wicked snarl. "I wish I had short hair like yours, Kay. This is going to take me a while. You should go ahead," Leah urged. "There's no need for both of us to be late."

"You're probably right. See you at the Academy, then," Kay said, practically sprinting out the door.

Once Leah was alone, the dream came back to her as if it were a vivid memory: it felt too real to be merely a dream. Leah had never believed in tea leaves and fortune-telling. But she couldn't help feeling that her dream was a premonition— one that ought to be heeded. Leah wanted to warn Alex, but she didn't know exactly what to warn her about.

After pulling a heavy sweater and her purple overalls on over her leotard and tights, Leah gathered up her dance bag and started down the stairs. Kay was most likely the best person for Leah to talk to about her dream. Leah hoped Kay would help her untangle its hidden meaning. Perhaps together they could make sense of it and save Alex from whatever danger lay ahead.

By Monday afternoon Leah felt completely worn out. Staying up late both Saturday and Sunday had been bad enough. But her early morning nightmare had ruined what little sleep Leah had managed to get.

As the dancers for the Bay Area Ballet mingled with the SFBA students warming up for their first full cast *Nutcracker* rehearsal, Leah found herself scanning the room for Alex. All day Leah had watched for the dark-haired Russian girl, afraid to let Alex out of her sight.

In the cafeteria during lunch Leah had tried to tell Kay about her dream. But first Linda, then Katrina, and finally Alex herself had joined them, making it impossible for Leah to get much past the beginning of the dream when the weather had changed. Kay probably thought Leah was losing her mind, getting so disturbed by the weather.

Leah was at the barre doing pliés to loosen her muscles when Patrick asked for everyone's attention.

"By now," Patrick began, "I think you should all have the gist of what I'm trying to do this year with *The Nutcracker*. My approach is not really as radical as some of you seem to think. I know nearly everyone here has been involved in some production of *The Nutcracker* somewhere at some time. What I'm asking is that you forget all that and allow yourselves to approach my choreography with an open mind."

Leah half expected Patrick to ask them if they'd completed his assignment, but he didn't. Instead, he began marking the various parts of the opening scene party with the different groups of dancers.

More than anything else that day, rehearsing the first act of *The Nutcracker* seemed to take Leah's mind off Alex and the political intrigue connected with the Kirov Ballet's visit. Leah could easily imagine everyone in their elegant satin party clothes, and finally, she actually felt as if she were at a party. Everyone else looked as though they were enjoying themselves, too. In fact, Leah realized the party they were pretending to have at the Stahlbaums was a lot like the party at the Lydgates Saturday night had been!

After running through the first act twice without stopping, Patrick declared the rehearsal a success.

"I won't pretend I'm not surprised," Patrick said at the end of rehearsal. "I am surprised. I expected to have to beat what I wanted out of you. I'm very pleased. Well done! Next time, on to the second act!" With that, Patrick applauded the class as they in turn applauded him.

Later, in the dressing room, Finola Darling suggested that their successful rehearsal merited a celebration. "My body is crying out for chocolate," Finola declared in her clipped British accent. "How about hitting Cocoa-Nuts, mates?"

"For dinner?" Kay asked, stuffing her wig into her dance bag. It had been the only part of her costume that Patrick insisted she wear. But poor

Kay had had a difficult time keeping it on her head while she danced full out, and it was beginning to look like Patrick might give in and let Kay dance the part of Clara without the wig.

"I don't know about the rest of you, but I've already missed dinner at my house," Katrina Gray pointed out. "Anyway, I can't think of anything I'd rather have for dinner than something gooey and ultra-fattening!"

"How about you, Alex?" Leah asked anxiously. She wanted to go along with her friends, but she had had an uneasy feeling about Alex all day long. Now that it was dark, Leah's concern had intensified. Furthermore, thinking about the role Mrs. Hanson's house had played in her dream made Leah want to postpone going back there as long as possible. Yet Leah didn't want to go anywhere without Alex.

Alex grinned. Obviously, there was nothing bothering her—in fact, quite the opposite. "Why not!" she cried, throwing her arms up into the air in a carefree gesture. "All work and nothing else makes one dull," she declared.

"That's 'All work and no play makes Jack a dull boy,' " Kay corrected Alex.

Giggling slightly, Alex said, "I do not know this Jack! I think I like my way better."

Finola nodded. "I like your way better, too, Alex."

As soon as Katrina finished braiding her hair, the five friends headed over to their favorite hangout, Cocoa-Nuts, although they didn't go there all that often. As much as each of the young dancers craved sweets, each knew that overindulging could cost her a career in ballet.

"I want a double fudge banana split," Finola announced as soon as the girls had claimed a table in the corner of the coffee shop.

"Is that what you're really going to have, Finola?" Kay asked, her voice full of envy. Since Kay was only five feet tall, she had to be even more careful about what she ate than the others.

"No," Finola said sadly. "It's only what I *want*. What I am going to have is a single scoop of chocolate ice cream."

"*I* am going to have a banana split," Alexandra declared greedily, handing back the menu the waitress had given her without even opening it.

Katrina, sitting on Alex's left, looked at the Russian girl as if she'd gone insane. "You're actually going to put away a week's worth of calories in one sitting? What will Patrick say if you don't fit into your snowflake costume tomorrow?"

Alex shrugged. "He will pace," she said, scowling in an imitation of Patrick. "He will call me fat thing. He will wave his arms," she added, waving her arms the way Patrick did when he was utterly frustrated. "Then he will have the wardrobe mistress let out my costume." Everyone laughed as Alex handed the waitress back her menu and said, "And much chocolate syrup, please."

"I'll have a large iced tea," Kay said with a sigh. "And go heavy on the lemon, please." As the waitress moved around the table to take Leah's order, Kay added, "I'm probably going to put on five pounds just looking at that banana split of yours, Alex. I wish I had your courage. You could probably really stand up to Robson if you had to. I know I couldn't even stand up to happy-go-lucky Patrick."

"Leah taught me something last night," Alex explained. "Nothing ventured, nothing gained."

Leah shook her head. "I wasn't talking about weight!" she insisted.

Everyone at the table laughed at that, Alex laughing the hardest ... and the loudest. In fact, Leah had never heard Alex laugh a loud, raucous laugh before. Leah told herself that it was probably a good sign. Alex needed to relax and have a good time, since everything going on around her was so stressful.

"I have an idea!" Alex announced as the laughter began to die down. "Someone ought to make a film of ballet rehearsals, you know, like that bloopers thing on television. It could be called *Great Ballet Bloopers*! Like today when Kay's wig came off and flew into Kenny's face so he could not see where he was going."

"Yes!" Alex hooted, her voice growing increasingly louder. "Or how about the first time the soldiers battled the mice? Did you not think the mice were going to win? And how about when Kay threw her slipper at the mouse king and hit Patrick in the head instead!"

As Finola and Katrina joined Alex in another round of laughter, Kay leaned close to Leah and started tugging urgently on the sleeve of Leah's purple sweatshirt.

"What is it?" Leah asked.

"How can we get Alex to stop?" Kay whispered.

"She's just releasing tension, that's all," Leah commented. "It's good for her."

"I don't think so," Kay replied. With a meaningful arch of her eyebrows, Kay indicated an attractive young man sitting a few tables away from them. He appeared to be alone, and from the way he was dressed, Leah guessed he was a college student. "We're being watched or, to put it more accurately, *Alex* is being watched," she whispered.

At Kay's urging, Leah examined the student a little more closely. There was no doubt he was watching Alex, but he hardly looked threatening. "I don't think he's a spy," Leah assured Kay. "He's just bored or something so he's watching Alex. After all, she *is* putting on a good show."

"That's my point!" Kay whispered a little more fiercely. "Alex is putting on *too* good a show. She's drawing entirely too much attention to herself. As soon as Alex speaks, it's obvious that she's Russian. If she didn't have that accent—"

"What are you two whispering about?" Finola demanded, leaning in front of Kay.

"Nothing," Kay said quickly, straightening up.

Finola's eyebrows shot up. "It certainly was something. Have you got a secret from the rest of us, or what?"

"Who's got a secret?" Katrina wanted to know.

Deciding that it was in Alex's best interest to say something, Leah said, "Kay was just talking about that boy over there."

"I say, Alex," Finola remarked, instantly spotting the boy in question. "I think that fellow fancies you over every dessert on the menu."

Alex gave the boy a quick glance before returning her attention to her half-eaten sundae. "He is cute," Alex observed offhandedly, plunging her spoon into the extra chocolate sauce she'd ordered. "But too bad for him, he is not my type."

"What *is* your type, then? I for one would be interested to know." Finola ran her spoon along the inside of her ice cream dish as she waited for Alex to answer.

"Did you see that?" Kay hissed into Leah's ear as Alex began listing the qualities she found admirable in a male. "That man just winked at Alex!"

"Calm down, Kay," Leah ordered. "What can he do in a public place like this, anyway? Besides, he's just a boy. I doubt if they let boys work for the KGB."

"Look again, Leah. He's *not* just a boy. He looks young because of his haircut, but if you look closely, you'll see that he's actually much older."

Kay was so flustered that Leah felt she'd better take another look at the guy. But when she turned around, he was gone.

"Relax, Kay." Leah patted the back of Kay's hand. "He left. That must mean he's not tailing us after all. He just found Alex attractive, that's all. When Alex didn't return his attention, he left."

"Maybe," Kay conceded, but she sounded doubtful.

Leah turned away from Kay and tried to join in Finola's conversation with Alex. It was undoubtedly Kay's paranoia, Leah now realized, that had made her have such an awful dream. It hadn't been a premonition—just a reaction to all of the hysterical nonsense Kay had been putting in her head. Leah had enough to think about at the moment with their performances of *The Nutcracker* coming up, and the Kirov coming to town, not to mention the dance history paper she'd barely begun working on. She didn't have time to worry about schemes of international espionage that didn't even exist!

"Tell us about Nureyev's *Nutcracker,* Finola,"

Leah pleaded. "I've heard about it, but you must have some inside information, being from the Royal Ballet School and all."

As Finola elaborated, Leah couldn't help but notice Kay staring at the door. Leah also noticed that Alex wasn't paying much attention to Finola's story, either. But instead of looking worried as Kay did, Alex looked dreamy-eyed. If Leah didn't know better, she'd have sworn at that moment that Alex was in love!

Chapter 8

Leah was startled to see the library lights flash on and off, signaling that the building would close in ten minutes. She had been so engrossed in reading about different productions of *The Nutcracker* for her dance history paper that somehow the evening had slipped away from her. Flipping the books closed and piling them into a neat stack, Leah headed for the main counter to check them all out.

"You're ambitious," Georgio Bennet commented. He was a second-year student at SFBA who worked at the school library as part of his scholarship.

Leah rolled her eyes. "What I really am is a procrastinator. I should have started this paper the minute it was assigned instead of putting it off until now."

Georgio nodded sympathetically. "It's hard enough trying to rehearse for *The Nutcracker* and keep up with classes at the same time. Now that the Kirov's here, it's even harder to get anything done. No one talks about anything else."

"Did you get tickets to a performance?" Leah asked.

Georgio nodded. "Tomorrow night. How about you?"

Leah smiled. The promise of seeing the Kirov
had been the one thing that had kept her going
all week. "We're going tomorrow night, too," she
said without thinking. Then Leah felt her face
instantly flush. Suppose Georgio should ask who
she was going with? She couldn't say she was
going with Alex in disguise!

Luckily Georgio merely stamped Leah's books
and handed them back to her without asking who
Leah meant by "we." "Usually you can have things
for two weeks. But because the holidays are coming up, you can have these only one week. Sorry,"
he explained.

"That's okay." Leah gathered up the books.
"Thanks."

"See you later," Georgio called after her.

As Leah walked out onto the street, she was
startled to find how dark it was, almost pitch
black. Fog had rolled in from the Bay, shrouding
everything in its murky dampness. There was, in
fact, something chillingly familiar about this awful weather. Suddenly, Leah's Monday-morning
dream came flooding back to her.

After looking nervously down the street, Leah
was tempted to go back into the library and call a
cab, even though her boardinghouse was just a
few blocks away. A foghorn sounded in the distance and Leah chuckled. What was she so afraid
of? A silly dream? The streets were well lit. Besides, a walk, even a short walk, might revive her
enough so that she could study some more before going to bed.

It was only ten o'clock, but it seemed more like
midnight. For one thing, there weren't very many
people out and about. Leah's footsteps echoed

eerily on the sidewalk, and she kept turning around to make sure no one was following her.

By the time Leah arrived at the street the boardinghouse was on, she was almost running. It wasn't the weight of the books she was carrying that was making her hurry, though they were heavy enough. It was the weight of the unknown! Despite everything Leah tried to tell herself, her dream still haunted her.

Finally, Leah saw the shadowy outline of Mrs. Hanson's. The boardinghouse had never looked better to her. Clutching her books tightly to her chest, Leah prepared to hurry the rest of the way down the street. Then she saw him!

Terrified, Leah came to a standstill and stared at the sinister figure leaning against the lamppost directly in front of the house. The man was obviously staring up at something or someone inside. And in the glow of the streetlight, Leah saw that something about this person was disturbingly familiar. Cautiously, Leah edged forward, trying to get a better look at him.

As she got closer, Leah saw that he was wearing a tan jacket and a matching cap. It was the kind of cap Leah had seen golfers wear in magazines. He was whistling softly, just under his breath. Leah didn't recognize the tune, but it was something in a minor key, something that sounded ... Russian!

All at once Leah realized it was the same guy who'd been staring at Alex the other night at Cocoa-Nuts! Leah shuddered as she finally saw just *what* he was looking at—Alex's second floor room. Even from where Leah stood, she could see

Alex's distinct outline against the sheer curtains covering the windows.

Leah's first thought was to run to the phone booth on the corner and call the police. But that, she realized, would be impossible to do without walking right past the man. Running into the house was a better idea, Leah decided. But while she was waiting for the right moment to make her move, Alex's light suddenly went out.

Having lost the object of his fascination, the man's head now turned in Leah's direction. Their eyes met, and Leah was certain that he recognized her as easily as she had recognized him. For a moment he just stared at Leah with his mouth open, looking stunned. Leah couldn't tell which of them was more frightened. Then the guy turned away and hurried down the street in the opposite direction.

Leah stood for a few seconds, too shaken to move. Then she, too, ran—right into Mrs. Hanson's boardinghouse. All Leah could think about as she burst through the front door was telling someone about the mysterious man. But the house was so quiet. Everyone seemed to be in bed already.

Overcome by indecision, Leah stood looking anxiously about the foyer. Whom should she tell, she asked herself. And what would she tell them? Was the guy a member of the KGB, waiting to kidnap Alex? Or was he just some crazy guy with an unhealthy interest in Alex, a Peeping Tom? What would or could the police do? And what could Madame Preston or Mrs. Hanson do but call the police?

Leah had just decided to talk the whole thing

over with Kay when the telephone on the hall table began to ring. Relieved by the familiar sound, Leah dove to pick up the receiver.

"Hello?" she said eagerly.

A few seconds of silence elapsed before a male voice said, "Is Alexandra there?"

"Alexandra!" Leah gasped before she could stop herself. Then, clearing her throat, she said more calmly, "Alex has gone to bed. Can I take a message?"

"This is her friend," the man said, acting as if he were the only friend Alex had. "Is this Leah Stephenson?"

"How did you know my name?" Leah demanded with a combination of anger and dread. "Who are you? Why are you calling here so late at night?" Leah knew she sounded hysterical but she couldn't help it.

"You leave message for me then!" the man said, responding to Leah's questions with a demand of his own. He had a strong Russian accent that Leah hadn't noticed at first.

"Look, you—" Leah began, feeling a little bolder. But the man cut her off before she could finish.

"You tell Miss Sorokin she meet me tomorrow, three P.M. sharp."

"Where?" Leah demanded shrilly.

"Alexandra knows where," the voice said coldly. "You must tell her when." Then there was a click, and Leah knew he had hung up.

The receiver felt like ice in Leah's hand as she stared at it, trying to decide what to do. Leah wanted to believe that she hadn't seen that guy out front, that the phone hadn't rung just now, that the voice on the phone hadn't had a Russian accent. But she knew it was real, all of it.

Finally, Leah set the receiver down. She had to talk to Kay right away. Only Kay had had a constant sense of foreboding about Alex and the KGB. Kay would believe Leah, there was no doubt in Leah's mind about that. Then the two of them could do whatever had to be done together.

Happy to have made a decision, Leah flew up the stairs to the second floor. Slowly, she opened the door to Kay's room. "Kay," she whispered into the dark. Leah didn't want to wake Linda, Kay's roommate, but sometimes Kay slept so soundly that only a good shake could rouse her.

"Leah?" Kay sat up and stared at her bedroom door. "That is you, isn't it? What's wrong?"

Leah sighed in relief. It was so good to hear Kay's voice, even if it was just a whisper.

"Come out here," Leah said, waving her arms frantically in the direction of the hall. "I've got to talk to you!" Leah stepped back into the hall and leaned against the wall. She could feel her heart pounding in her chest.

"Leah, what is it?" Kay asked, slipping her arms into the sleeves of her red flannel robe as she joined Leah in the hall.

"Not here," Leah said. She glanced furtively in both directions. "Someone might hear us."

"How about your room, then?" Kay suggested.

Leah shook her head. Her room didn't feel safe, either. Remembering the guy under the streetlight, Leah didn't want to be in any room that faced the front of the house.

"I know," Leah said. "The back stairway. No one ever uses it. We can talk privately there."

"Leah, everyone's in bed," Kay pointed out. But she followed Leah, anyway.

"I'm not sure where to start," Leah began once the girls were safely sequestered on the narrow stairway.

"Start at the beginning," Kay urged her.

Leah took a deep breath, then slowly exhaled. "Well, that guy from Cocoa-Nuts, you know, the one you thought might be from the KGB?"

Kay blushed as she nodded. "I have been a little bit nuts this week, haven't I? I guess it's all the pressure of rehearsals."

"Listen to me, Kay," Leah whispered. "You were right to be suspicious of that guy. He wasn't just flirting with Alex that night."

"What do you mean, Leah?" Kay asked.

"That same guy was lurking outside the board-inghouse just now when I came home! He was staring up at Alex's room, just watching her—it was so creepy."

Kay's deep blue eyes widened in surprise. "Where is he now? Is he still out there?"

Leah shook her head. "He saw me and ran away. But then, when I came in, the phone rang. Some guy with a Russian accent asked for Alex. He said she had to meet him tomorrow. He even knew *my* name, can you believe it?"

"Leah, that's awful!" Kay cried. She grabbed hold of Leah's hands and squeezed them tightly. "Was it the guy out front who called?"

"I don't know," Leah said. "The guy outside never said anything. But it does seem like a strange coincidence, doesn't it? The guy runs away and immediately the phone rings. What should I do, Kay? Should I call Madame Preston or what? I thought about calling the police, but what would I say? And what could they do, anyway?"

"We have to think this over carefully," Kay told Leah, for once the more organized of the two. "If we call Madame Preston, Alex isn't going to be able to go to the ballet tomorrow night with us, you know," Kay pointed out.

"But isn't Alex's safety more important than the ballet?" Leah asked.

"Yes, but maybe it doesn't have to be one or the other. Maybe *we* can protect Alex somehow, so that she can see the Kirov and be safe at the same time." Kay leaned back against the wall, narrowing her eyes thoughtfully. "Together we must be able to come up with a plan."

Leah shook her head. "I don't know, Kay. You didn't see that man out there staring up at Alex's window. Then that voice ... it was so scary. I'm afraid this is more than we can handle."

"Maybe it's too much for one person—but not for two. And don't forget, this is Alex's problem, too. And you know how she's been lately," Kay reminded Leah. "If we ruin her opportunity to see the Kirov without at least consulting her, she's going to be furious."

Leah sighed. "You're right about that. I guess we should wake Alex up and tell her everything."

Kay nodded as she stifled a yawn. "But let's talk to her in the morning. Nothing is going to happen to her before tomorrow, anyway. Right?"

"Right. And I'm sure Alex is sound asleep by now," Leah agreed. "Maybe everything will seem different in the morning after a good night's sleep."

Getting to her feet, Kay said, "Maybe. Well, good night, Leah."

"Good night," Leah responded. Kay headed back to her room, and Leah climbed the stairs to the third floor.

Without turning the light on in her room, Leah slipped out of her clothes and into her nightgown. She hoped the mysterious man was no longer watching the house.

Was Alex in danger, Leah wondered. Was someone trying to kidnap her, or had the guy out front and the weird phone call been merely coincidences? As Leah slipped between the cool sheets on her bed, she wished that the Kirov had already come and gone. With everything that was going on, having the famous company in town for a few days seemed like a threat instead of a treat.

Chapter 9

*Leah woke up with an anxious feel-*ing in the pit of her stomach; she had to talk to Alex right away! It was Friday, the day Alex was supposed to attend the Kirov performance with Kay and Leah. Alex had to be told as soon as possible about the phone call and the man who'd been watching her, so she could decide what to do. After quickly pulling on her clothes, Leah grabbed her dance bag and practically flew out the door.

Downstairs, Leah knocked on Alex's door. But there was no answer. "Alex!" Leah called, knocking again.

"Alex is on the phone," Kay told Leah, sticking her head into the hall. Kay was alternately squirting her curly hair with water and then rubbing the curls briskly with a towel.

Leah walked into Kay's room and sat down on her bed. "Do you know who she's talking to?"

Kay shrugged. "Nope. I do know that she doesn't seem very upset, though. In fact, the last time I looked to see if she was still talking, she was grinning."

"Maybe it's her mother or Andrei or someone like that," Leah suggested.

"Maybe," Kay said.

Then, draping her damp towel over her desk chair, Kay gave her curly head a final shake. "Well, I'm all set," she declared, picking up her bag and slinging it over her shoulder. "After that late night conversation of ours, I'm going to need some hot tea to get me going. How does that sound? We have a few minutes."

"Hot tea sounds great," Leah agreed. "I hope Alex gets off the phone soon. We really have to talk to her right away, you know. Maybe we could talk to her over tea."

When the girls got downstairs, however, Alex was still on the phone. Leah and Kay paused a few feet from the spot where Alex was sitting, her long legs propped lazily on the banister. Alex glanced suspiciously at them out of the corner of her eye. Then, covering the mouthpiece with one hand, she said, "Yes? You girls wanted something of me?"

Leah and Kay exchanged glances. "Yes," Leah answered. "We just thought you might want some tea before class. Kay and I would like to talk to you about something important."

Alex shook her head. "I cannot talk now. I am busy. We talk later." Then she took her hand away from the receiver and continued her phone conversation. Only now Alex's voice was much softer, almost a whisper. Blushing a little, Leah felt once again as if *she* were the spy.

"Come on, then," Kay said, urging Leah to follow her to the kitchen. "We just have to talk to Alex later, that's all."

Leah nodded and followed Kay.

They were just sitting down at the large kitchen table when Pam walked into the room. Immediately, Pam launched into one of her tales about the way *The Nutcracker* ought to be done which was, of course, the way it was done in Atlanta. When Pam started telling them how gorgeous her wavy red hair had looked, loose and flowing about her shoulders when she had danced the role of Clara as a child of eleven, Leah decided it was time for them to leave. As they slipped out of the kitchen into the front hall, Pam kept talking to Abby, who'd arrived just as Pam had begun her boring discourse. Out in the front hallway, Alex was still talking away as well.

"You're going to be late if you don't get off the phone," Kay warned as the girls passed Alex.

But Alex only made a silly face and waved Kay and Leah dismissively in the direction of the door.

"You know," Kay said as the girls started walking toward the Academy, "Alex has the strangest attitude lately. It's almost as if she wishes she weren't here anymore."

"I was thinking the same thing myself," Leah said. "It's like she finds everything about SFBA sort of boring—including us. In fact, I think Alex might even be enjoying the danger she's in! Alex and I had a conversation last week in my room. I think I might have told you about it already. Anyway, I was so wrapped up in my own problems that I didn't pay as much attention to what she was saying as I should have. Now little snatches of that conversation keep coming back to haunt me."

"So, what did Alex say?" Kay demanded.

"She told me she was feeling like a bird in a cage. She's been feeling like she needs a break from the routine of SFBA, from the routine of a dancer's life. It isn't going to be easy, Kay, but we're going to have to be extra careful for Alex's sake. I just don't think she realizes the seriousness of this situation."

"I agree," Kay said. "Think maybe we should go back and wait for her?"

Leah shook her head. "We can't just stand over Alex until she gets off the phone—then she'll get mad and she won't talk to us at all." Leah held the large front door of the mansion that served as the San Francisco Ballet Academy open for Kay.

"Thanks. We'll just have to try approaching Alex in the dressing room before class, I guess."

Leah agreed to that. But Alex never showed up in the dressing room. When the girls finally went to the studio for class, Alex wasn't there, either.

After joining the others for warm-up stretches on the floor, Leah and Kay anxiously watched the door for the arrival of their Russian friend. Then, all at once, Madame swept into the room and began clapping her hands for the students to find their places at the barre. Leah and Kay exchanged worried glances. It was beginning to look as if Alex were about to commit one of the worst offenses at SFBA, arriving late for Madame Preston's class!

Madame was already up to battements tendus when a sheepish-looking Alex slipped into the studio. Madame simply pretended not to notice Alex, who quickly found an opening at the barre. But Leah knew that Madame had seen Alex: something as glaring as arriving nearly seven minutes late for Alicia Preston's class just didn't go unnoticed. Besides, a fierceness had entered Madame's steely gray eyes that hadn't been there before.

Leah half expected Madame to stop the class

and reprimand Alex, but she didn't. Instead, the SFBA's regal director moved on to the next exercise. With Alex directly in front of Leah, Leah couldn't help but watch her. Amazingly, the Russian girl seemed to be having no trouble, even though she couldn't possibly be warmed up, having missed the pliés and tendus that routinely began any morning class.

The students were all the way to their adagio work when Madame rapped the top of the baby grand piano impatiently, signaling Robert to stop playing.

"Alexandra Sorokin!" Madame said fiercely. "You have been a beat off since you first wandered in here. Being a dancer means learning discipline. Lately, I think you have forgotten the meaning of that word!"

Madame glared at Alex. But Alex didn't look away the way Leah knew she herself would have. Instead, the dark-haired girl glared back at her teacher with a look every bit as stern as Madame's.

"What," Madame finally said, "would your parents say if they could see you this very minute, Miss Sorokin?" Then, without waiting for Alex's reply, Madame Preston signaled Robert to resume playing.

Leah was shocked. Madame was known for her corrections. Madame's astute corrections were, in fact, the reason everyone from both the company and the school wanted to attend her monthly Sunday morning class. Ruthless as Alicia Preston's corrections were, they were always perceived as fair, at least in the long run.

But Madame's attack on Alex this morning seemed to Leah totally unfair. She had made no specific comment, instead, she had brought Alex's *parents* into the whole matter. That seemed, to Leah, doubly unjust.

Madame Preston, of all people, should understand the strain Alex was under, Leah told herself. Alex needed to be given extra support; she certainly didn't need to be attacked.

During the early part of their center work, Madame singled out Alex again and again for minor corrections. Her alignment was off. Her weight was thrown back on her hip. Her rear end was sticking out. Madame even complained that Alex's appearance was sloppy! But compared with Madame's comment about Alex's parents, it all seemed tame.

When class was over and the girls began heading to the dressing room, Leah lingered in the studio a moment, hoping to give Alex a consoling word or two. But Alex didn't seem to notice that Leah was waiting for her. As soon as Alex had gathered up her discarded leg warmers and shawl, she trooped after the other girls toward the dressing room.

"What did you think of that?" Kay asked, catching up to Leah in the hall outside the dressing room.

Leah shook her head. "I don't know what to think. I only know we've got to talk to Alex, Kay. Now!"

"Come on then," Kay said, reaching for the dressing room door. "This may be our only chance to talk to Alex before the Kirov's performance tonight."

"... And then again this morning," Pam was saying pointedly to Abigail as Kay and Leah entered the dressing room.

"The same guy?" Abigail said, winding her

mouse-brown hair into a knot at the back of her head.

"It sounded like the same guy to me," Pam said in her heaviest southern drawl. "Was it, Alex?" she asked over her shoulder. "Or have you got an entourage of male admirers calling our little ol' boardinghouse morning, noon, and night?"

Leah couldn't believe that Pam had the insensitivity to be *teasing* Alex after the terrible treatment she'd just received from Madame Preston during class! Worried, Leah looked over at Alex to see how she was taking Pam's comments, prepared to leap to Alex's defense if necessary.

But Alexandra's face looked about as expressive as a stone. She was raking her comb through her waist-long dark hair with extraordinary zeal, but she seemed more excited than angry.

"I guess if I were as popular as you've suddenly become with the opposite sex," Pam persisted, "I'd skip my pliés, too. You're probably finding other ways to warm up." Abigail giggled and Pam smiled triumphantly at her own reflection in the mirror.

Feeling outraged on Alex's behalf, Leah opened her mouth to tell Pam to mind her own business. But before Leah could get the first word out, Alex spun around and faced Pam.

"Mind your own business, Pamela Hunter!" Alex snapped. She gave her glossy black hair a haughty toss. "In fact," Alex added, her ebony eyes sparkling as she looked around the room, taking in every girl present, "*all* of you must mind your own business! This is a free country, is it not? I am free to live my own life. Leave me alone!" Alex said, her voice rising with obvious passion.

Then after a brief pause, she added wearily, "Madame Preston must mind her own business, too, I think!" With that, she scooped up her things and started toward the door, leaving Leah—and, surprisingly, Pam—speechless.

"Alex, wait!" Kay called after her. Then she bravely followed Alex out of the dressing room.

"What was *that* all about?" Pam asked, turning to Abigail.

"I think Alex has gone off the deep end," Abigail said, shaking her head. "She can't even take a little teasing. She should be grateful that you've been answering the phone all the time for her. But no, not Alexandra Sorokin. She can't even say a simple thank-you to anyone."

"Didn't you hear what Alex said?" Leah said, leaping to her absent friend's defense. "Or is it just impossible for you two to mind your own business? Your lives must be pretty dull to pick on someone when they're down."

Pam snorted unpleasantly, and Leah found herself wondering, not for the first time, either, how anyone so beautiful could be so mean. "Look who's calling the kettle black, Abigail."

"What do you mean?" Leah demanded.

"Come on, Leah," Katrina said, attempting to guide Leah out of the dressing room by the arm. "Don't get into it with Pam, it isn't worth it."

But Alex *was* worth it; she was one of Leah's best friends, and Leah knew that Alex would stand up for her if the tables were turned.

"Pam, I asked you a question," Leah said.

"I'm not blind, you know," Pam said. "I've seen you and Kay sneaking around at all hours, peek-

ing into a certain Russian girl's room, holding
tête-à-têtes on the back stairs."

"You've been spying on us!" Leah cried.

Pam rolled her eyes. "You're a funny one to be
talking about spies, Leah Stephenson."

Leah had heard enough. Gathering up her dance
bag, she stormed from the dressing room.

"Leah!" Kay called, running up to her from
behind in the hallway. "Wait for me!"

"Did you get to talk to Alex? What did she
say?" Leah asked, turning around.

"She was kind of upset about the ribbing Pam
was giving her. But then, I guess you probably
could see that. Anyway, I told her about the guy
from Cocoa-Nuts and that phone call last night.
She sort of brushed it off, saying I shouldn't worry.
Then Alex told me not to say anything to anyone
about it—especially Madame Preston. So I gave
her my wig and her ticket for the ballet tonight.
She's going to meet us by the side door of the
Opera House right before the performance. That
way, she said, we won't have to hang out in the
lobby, where someone might come over to talk to
us. Oh, and she also said to tell you, 'Thank you
for everything!' "

Leah hung her dance bag in her school locker
and pulled out the loose-leaf notebook she'd need
for her first academic class of the day. "Thank
you for everything?" she repeated questioningly.
"That sounds so final."

"Well, it didn't sound that way when she said it.
She's really excited about seeing the Kirov tonight, thanks to us. But she's also pretty upset
about what happened this morning. First Madame,
then Pam and Abigail ..."

Leah sighed. "I wish Pam weren't the one with the first floor bedroom. She seems to know a lot about all these phone calls Alex has been getting. I'd like to know who's calling, but I'm not about to ask Pam to tell me. Alex has sure kept quiet about things lately."

"She's just been busy. We've all been busy," Kay insisted.

"Well, I just hope we're not putting Alex in any more danger by bringing her with us tonight," Leah commented.

"Relax," Kay told Leah. "Alex herself said she'd be safer at the Opera House than she would be back at the boardinghouse, all by herself. Everyone's going to see the Kirov tonight—even Mrs. Hanson."

For once Kay sounded cool and rational. Leah wanted to believe that Alex would be safe with them. But even more than that, she wanted to find out what was really going on with Alex.

Chapter 10

"Are you sure this is where we're supposed to meet Alex?" Leah asked, pulling her purple shawl around her shoulders. As usual, the San Francisco night air was cold and damp.

"I'm more than sure," Kay said. "Alex specifically said to meet her right here, by the side door. If it had been up to me, I would have had us meet inside the Opera House at our seats." Kay peered anxiously out at the darkness surrounding the building.

Leah could see that Kay was as nervous about Alex as she was. It was nearly eight o'clock, curtain time for the Kirov Ballet's performance of *Swan Lake.*

"Did you see Alex again after we talked?" Leah asked Kay eagerly.

Kay shook her head. "No. But I just remembered something! Linda mentioned she'd seen Alex late this afternoon at the boardinghouse."

"What time?"

"Linda said it was a little before three o'clock. She also said Alex seemed to be in a big hurry. I guess Linda tried to talk to her about Madame's class this morning, but Alex kind of gave her the brush-off," Kay answered.

"Three o'clock?" Leah cried. "Oh, no!"

"What's wrong?" Kay asked, grabbing Leah's arm.

"That man on the phone ... I forgot all about three o'clock!"

Kay gave Leah a little shake. "Tell me what you're talking about, Leah."

"The man who called last night said that Alex was supposed to meet him at three o'clock. And when I asked *where* she was supposed to meet him, he said Alex already knew that!"

"But if Alex already knew that ..." Kay began, her eyes as big as saucers.

"Exactly!" Leah exclaimed, slowly nodding her head as if everything finally made sense to her. "In order for Alex to know where to meet that man, she had to have talked to him before."

"Oh, my gosh!" Kay said, raising her hand to her mouth. "Maybe that man is the man who Alex has been talking to all week, the man Pam was teasing her about!"

"Kay? I'm afraid Alex is planning to go back to the Soviet Union."

"What?" Kay said, her face registering both shock and disbelief. "You can't be saying what I think you're saying."

"But what other explanation can there be?" Leah demanded, placing her hands on her hips. "Don't you see, Kay? This explains everything: the funny way Alex has been acting, the phone calls, even the strange way she reacted to Madame this morning. I know Alex has been upset about not being invited to join a company yet. I'm sure you heard that she has to audition as though she were just anybody for the Bay Area Ballet Company even though she's been at SFBA for the past three years. She's probably mad about being treated like that—after all, Alex was the recipient of the Golden Gate Award her first year at SFBA. And everyone in the ballet world knows that her parents are the renowned Olga and Dimitri Sorokin. Maybe that counts for something with the Kirov. Remember when she told us that the Kirov held the secret of her dance? She probably wants to dance with them."

Kay shook her head. "Do you suppose she knows what she's giving up?"

"I only wish I'd thought of all this sooner," Leah said as the deep conversation she'd had with Alex just a short time ago came flooding back into her mind. Leah could think of a million reasons why she didn't pay more attention to what she now saw as her friend's plea for help. There'd been that modeling assignment Leah had gotten herself involved with. Then there'd been the opportunity to star in the movie *Temptations* with James Cummings and Andrei, and Leah had been trying to make up her mind about it. Also, there had been *The Nutcracker* auditions that Leah had finally missed out on altogether. But none of her excuses seemed very valid at the moment.

If Leah hadn't been so wrapped up in herself, she might have listened better. Now, Alex, who already felt like a caged bird, was about to step from one cage into another. Leah wondered if Alex understood that her new cage would be locked as soon as she stepped into it, and perhaps never opened again.

"I think we should go into the Opera House, Leah," Kay said, breaking into Leah's thoughts. "Maybe Alex got here before we did and decided not to wait outside. Maybe she's already in her seat. She has her ticket, you know. I gave it to her this morning after class."

"Okay." Leah sighed. She was reluctant to even hope for a miracle like that. "Let's go in."

Leah followed Kay to the row of large glass doors that marked the front entrance of the War Memorial Opera House. As they entered the formal-looking lobby with its plush red carpeting and enormous crystal chandelier, Leah sighed.

Leah usually felt a tingle of excitement whenever she entered the Opera House. It had seemed like a dream come true that she was actually part of such fairy-tale splendor, and she still found it hard to believe that she'd danced on the Opera House stage before and would be dancing there again when *The Nutcracker* opened. But tonight Leah was far too upset to feel any tingle. Tonight the dream seemed like a nightmare.

"Look, Leah!" Kay cried, giving Leah a quick jab in the ribs. "Over there!"

Hoping against hope that Kay had spotted Alex amid the glamorous Opera House crowd, Leah looked where Kay was pointing. But instead of Alex, Leah saw an old man in a black opera cape and a black felt hat. The wide brim of the hat was pulled down so that it almost concealed the eye patch that covered the man's right eye.

Leah's first thought was of Alex's safety. This strange man, Leah feared, was yet another sinister figure in pursuit of her friend. Then Leah realized that there was something familiar about this oddly dressed person, something about his bold yet graceful movements that she'd seen before.

"Leah, it's Andrei," Kay whispered.

"You're right, it *is*," Leah said softly. She started toward the caped figure, but then stopped, remembering that Andrei had also been forbidden to attend this performance.

"Why are you stopping?" Kay demanded crossly. "Let's go get him and tell him what's happening. Maybe he can help us!"

Leah shook her head. "We better check inside first. We'll get Andrei in trouble if we blow his cover, and he'll be really mad at us if we do and Alex turns out to be okay."

"Uh-oh!" Kay said, turning abruptly in the opposite direction and pulling Leah with her. "I just saw Pam and Abby. We better go in before they come over to talk to us."

"I don't want to talk to those two right now, either," Leah agreed.

The girls had turned in their tickets and were starting down the aisle that the usher had directed them to when Kay said quietly, "I'm glad that Andrei's here. It makes me feel safer."

"Andrei being here doesn't necessarily mean Alex is safe and sound," Leah pointed out. "In fact, if Alex decided to go with the Soviets of her own accord, I'm not sure there's anything anyone can do, including Andrei Levintoff."

"I still find it really hard to believe that Alex would even think twice about returning to Russia. In fact, I'll bet you a pair of pink tights that Alex is already sitting down," Kay predicted optimistically. "When we tell her what we've been worrying about, I'm sure the three of us will have a good laugh together."

But when the girls finally located their seats,

Alex's was conspicuously empty. Kay's brave smile crumpled. "I was wrong, Alex *isn't* here! What if I was wrong about *everything*? Maybe Alex didn't decide to go back to Russia on her own. I mean, maybe she's been *brainwashed*. They probably promised Alex all sorts of things they might never even deliver, like leading roles in classic ballets!"

"Shhh!" A nicely dressed man in front of them motioned for Leah and Kay to quiet down. Unable to decide what to do next, Leah watched helplessly as the lights began to dim. The American and Russian anthems were played, and the orchestra began the first hauntingly beautiful strains of Tchaikovsky's famous score for *Swan Lake*.

As the ballet opened on Prince Siegfried's twenty-first birthday, it was impossible for Leah to pay attention. Her thoughts kept drifting back to Alex. Even when the Russians were dancing the famous first act pas de trois Leah herself had danced in a student production earlier in the year, Leah couldn't concentrate the way she had intended to. Where, Leah kept asking herself over and over again, was Alex? And what, if anything, could be done to help her now?

When the evil magician, Von Rothbart, made his entrance, Kay grabbed Leah's sleeve. Deciding Kay must really be caught up in the story of *Swan Lake*, Leah ignored her. But Kay tugged Leah's arm until Leah was finally forced to look at her petite friend. Instead of looking at the stage, Kay's deep blue eyes were fixed somewhere to her left. Her rosy cheeks were totally drained of color, as if she'd seen a ghost.

Leah scanned the audience, wondering what had upset Kay so much. Then she saw him—the same man who'd been lurking outside the board-inghouse the night before, the man from Cocoa-Nuts!

Wearing a well-cut, expensive suit, he looked much older than he had either of the other two times Leah had seen him. There was no question in her mind now that this guy was no young boy, no Peeping Tom. He simply had to be a member of the KGB.

"What does it mean?" Kay gasped, causing the man in front of them to make a shushing noise again.

Leah shrugged. "I'm not sure," she whispered as softly as she could. "Hopefully, it means Alex is all right. If he's here and she's not, then we know Alex isn't with him, right?"

"*If* he's the one who phoned," Kay countered. "But maybe there's more than one agent involved."

As soon as the houselights came on for the intermission, Kay suggested they find Andrei. It was time, she told Leah, for them to put Alex's safety first. Andrei would want them to even if it meant the three of them got in trouble.

But hard as the girls searched, they were un-able to find a trace of Andrei. As the houselights flashed on and off to signal the beginning of the second act, Kay said, "Let's go back to the board-inghouse, Leah. I'm not watching the ballet, any-way. I'm too worried about Alex. I guess I'm worried about Andrei now, too."

Leah shook her head. "I think we should stay here as long as that KGB man stays here." Leah inclined her head meaningfully in the direction of the man from Cocoa-Nuts who was still sitting across the aisle from them. "I think he may be waiting for Alex to meet us. Maybe she even spotted that guy here—maybe she came in before we did, saw him, and left the Opera House altogether."

Kay seemed to consider Leah's words. "You mean, maybe Alex *was* going to go back to Russia with him, but she changed her mind at the last minute?"

Leah nodded. "It's possible, isn't it?"

"I suppose it is possible," Kay concluded. "Oh, Leah, I hope you're right."

"I do, too," Leah told her sincerely.

But as the houselights dimmed again, Leah felt completely on edge. Carefully, she glanced to the left to check on the man from Cocoa-Nuts. But he wasn't looking at the stage; he was looking right at Leah. And when their eyes met, he winked!

Instantly, Leah knew she'd made a mistake. The man wasn't waiting for Alex, not this time. He was watching Kay and Leah! Maybe he knew they would try to prevent Alex from returning to Russia, and his mission was to keep them away from Alex until it was too late to save her.

Leah considered leaping up and dashing out of the theater, but the ballet had already begun again. There was absolutely no way to leave without causing an enormous stir. Besides, the man would only follow them and stop them from interfering.

If Leah and Kay wanted to help Alex, they would have to keep their wits about them, Leah realized. They would have to act slowly and thoughtfully, and they would have to lose the KGB man before they did anything.

As soon as the performance ended, Leah urged Kay to hurry out of the theater. The Kirov was still bowing to the crowd's thunderous applause, while roses rained down on them from the balcony, when Leah and Kay slipped through the large glass doors into the damp December night.

Once they were outside, Kay said, "What is it, Leah?"

"That guy from Cocoa-Nuts winked at me," Leah replied, trying her hardest to remain calm. "I think he was at the ballet tonight to watch *us*. I think he knew Alex wouldn't be there with us. I also think he wants to keep us away from Alex until they have her safely tucked away. You were right, Kay. The Soviets have brainwashed Alex into going back to Russia with them. She probably thinks she'll be better off there. We've got to find her, Kay."

Leah directed her dainty friend toward the row of waiting cabs parked along the curb in front of the Opera House. After a quick glance backward to make sure they weren't being followed, Leah said, "I think we should take separate cabs, Kay. Make the driver take an indirect route back to Mrs. Hanson's. I'll meet you there."

Kay didn't protest. Merely nodding in agreement, Kay quickly hopped into the nearest cab. Leah got into a cab several cars behind Kay's, and when the two cabs took off, it was in opposite directions.

Leah had her cab drop her off a block away from the boardinghouse. As she cautiously approached Mrs. Hanson's, she heard a loud "Pssst!" from the doorway of the neighboring row house.

Afraid it was the man she was trying to escape, Leah ran by and hurried up the steps to Mrs. Hanson's. After hastily unlocking the front door, Leah slipped inside. Once the door was locked behind her, she leaned back against the curtained glass and sighed. She could feel her heart pounding in her chest as she struggled to take deep breaths.

"Leah!" someone croaked from within the house.

Leah practically jumped out of her skin. Then she realized it was Kay. "Kay, you just about scared me to death!"

"I came in the back," Kay explained apologetically. "I didn't mean to scare you."

"Was that you in the doorway next door?" Leah managed to ask. Kay nodded and Leah sighed with relief. "Thank goodness! I was afraid that KGB guy had followed us back here. Come on, then. Let's check Alex's room. If there's any sign of a struggle up there, we should contact Madame right away."

Kay nodded and the girls started up the stairs to Alex's room. As Leah flicked on the overhead light, the happy, vivid colors that Alex had decorated her room with greeted them mockingly.

"She's not here," Kay said, stating the obvious.

"Did you expect her to be?" Leah asked, heading straight for Alex's closet.

Kay shrugged. "I guess not."

"Look!" Leah exclaimed, stepping back so Kay could see inside. "At least half of everything that Alex owns is gone!"

"You mean ..." Kay began.

But Leah wouldn't let her finish. "Alex has packed her clothes and left! You know what this means, don't you?"

Again Kay nodded. "It means you were right, Leah. Alex has chosen to go back to Russia. I guess you don't clean your room and pack your favorite things when you're being kidnapped."

"No, not when you're being kidnapped," Leah agreed. "But maybe when you've been *brainwashed*!"

Sinking down on Alex's bright orange bedspread, Kay said, "Then we're too late, aren't we?"

"Maybe not," Leah said forcefully. "Maybe we still have time to stop them!"

"But how!" Kay demanded. "We don't have any idea where they are."

"No, we don't, but maybe Andrei Levintoff does," Leah suggested.

"Andrei? You don't think Andrei is in on this, do you?" Kay asked, wide-eyed.

"No," Leah admitted, "I don't. But Andrei's Russian, and he did defect just recently. He must know how these things work. You know, who's involved and all that. I bet Andrei even knows that agent who's been watching all of us—the one at the Opera House tonight."

"Okay," Kay said, "let's call him."

"I think it would be better to talk to him in person. Who knows, the phone here might even be bugged. Besides, Andrei will have to listen to us in person. We've got to hurry," Leah added.

"I'm ready," Kay said solemnly, her chin level and her gaze steady. Kay had really risen to this crisis, Leah noted.

Seeing Kay gathered together the way she was made Leah's own inner strength and stamina rise to the surface. She and Kay were going to save Alex, and that was all there was to it!

"I have a plan," Leah said. "But first we'll need to change into some warm dark clothes, and I'll have to figure out a way to cover up my blond hair. Come on, let's go to my room!"

Chapter 11

After pulling on the navy blue beret that completed her dark outfit, Leah said, "We better get going, Kay. Everyone will be coming back from the Opera House soon."

As Kay and Leah stepped out of the boarding-house to head for Andrei's apartment, Leah heard the unmistakable whine of Abigail Handardt's voice. Quickly, Leah pulled Kay into the shadows along the front of the house, where their dark clothes hid them from view.

"I couldn't believe it, Pam," Abigail said as the twosome walked right past Kay and Leah on their way up Mrs. Hanson's front walk. "I know the Kirov is supposed to have some of the best dancers in the world, but *you* were much better in the first act pas de trois of *Swan Lake* than that Russian girl who danced your part tonight."

Kay and Leah exchanged incredulous looks. *Pam's* part, Abby had said, as if the dance had been originally choreographed on the redhead from Atlanta!

Once Pam and Abby were safely inside the boardinghouse, Leah said, "Shall we take a cab? It would be the fastest thing to do."

Kay shook her head. "After that last cab, I'm broke."

"I'm low on funds myself," Leah confessed, hustling Kay toward the corner. "We'll have to take the bus to Andrei's place, then. My treat. It won't be as fast, but it'll be faster than walking."

Fortunately, they didn't have to wait long for a bus. But the relief that Leah had felt at having a bus arrive so quickly was short-lived. After she'd dropped her change into the box, Leah noticed something odd about the other four passengers. They weren't sitting together, but they were dressed exactly alike! Their coats were dark green wool and had the same style lapels. Their hats were trimmed in the same black fur—the famous Russian sable, Leah realized with a jolt!

Quickly, Leah took a seat. As she joined Leah, Kay said, "Is something wrong, Leah? You look as if you've seen a ghost."

"Don't turn around, Kay," Leah said softly.

"Why not?" Kay demanded, glancing over her shoulder.

"I told you not to turn around," Leah whispered, poking Kay in the ribs. "This bus is full of Russians."

Despite Leah's warning, Kay turned again. "Leah, everyone is wearing matching coats and hats," she observed.

"No kidding! We've got to get off this bus," Leah said.

"But won't they follow us just like that Kabuki couple did?"

"They weren't really following us," Leah reminded her. "We just thought they were because we were going to the same place." Then it dawned on her that perhaps she and Kay were going to the same place as these Russian spies—Andrei Levintoff's apartment.

Alarmed by her own suspicions, Leah said, "The next time the bus stops, we'll both jump off as quickly as we can. You go to the right, I'll go to the left. Duck out of sight, count to ten, then come out and I'll meet you. We'll walk the rest of the way. Got it?" Leah asked.

"Got it!" Kay said so loudly that Leah cringed. Nervously, Leah looked out the window and tried to catch the reflection of the people behind her to see if they'd been listening. But none of them seemed to be paying the slightest bit of attention to the girls. Instead, everyone was staring out their respective windows at the dark December night.

When the bus lurched to a stop, Leah gave Kay a nudge, pushing her into the aisle. Kay stood up, and Leah did likewise. Leah followed Kay off the bus, but so, Leah noticed in horror, did the four people she suspected were Russians!

As the bus pulled away, Leah saw Kay had immediately forgotten their plan of action. She took hold of Kay's sleeve and practically dragged her across the street. Together they started walking up Market toward Van Ness.

The Russians went in all four possible directions at the intersection, so that only one of them was left walking up Market Street in the same direction as the girls. Leah slowed her pace, curious to see if the green-coated figure across the street from them would match their steps.

What followed was like some crazy modern ballet. One moment Leah thought the other person was going to go on up the street at a healthy clip. But suddenly he, too, slowed down. Leah slowed down more, and so did the Russian.

Leah pulled Kay to the other side of the street. Then the man crossed to the opposite side. Feeling she was in charge of their little game of cat-and-mouse made Leah bolder and bolder. Leah quickened the pace again, then stopped altogether and turned around.

"What's going on, Leah?" Kay demanded.

"I'm trying to see if he's following us or if we're following him," Leah replied, scanning first one side of the street and then the other.

"Are *we* following *him*?" Kay asked. "I thought we wanted to lose them all."

"I did, too. But now I don't know," Leah confessed, feeling more confused than ever. "If they don't want us to follow them, they must be trying to hide something from us. Like Alex's whereabouts, for instance. I thought they were going to Andrei's like us. But maybe they're on their way to wherever they've got Alex stashed."

"Well, we've lost him now," Kay pointed out, waving her arm at the empty sidewalk on both sides of the street. "Or he's lost us! Whatever!"

Leah shrugged. "We might as well go on to Andrei's. I don't like this at all, Kay. Everything keeps changing all the time. First I'm certain this is what's really going on, then it turns out I'm wrong. It's like some weird dream or something."

Kay nodded. "Like Clara's dream in *The Nutcracker*, where the mice turn out to be her parents' guests when she wakes up!" Kay exclaimed. "Only then Drosselmeyer winks at her like it wasn't a dream after all!"

When Leah and Kay finally reached Van Ness, Leah thought she spotted a green-coated figure dart into a building up the street. Then she thought she saw another green-coated figure farther down on the other side of the street. But maybe, Leah told herself, she was only seeing things. She decided not to say anything to Kay about the flashes of dark green that kept appearing in front of her. There was no need for both of them to worry about what could very well turn out to be a mirage.

Finally they arrived in front of Andrei's apartment building just off Van Ness. To Leah's great relief, she saw that Andrei's third floor corner apartment was lit up like a Christmas tree.

"He's home!" Leah exclaimed joyously. "I was afraid after all this that he wouldn't be," she added, hurrying toward the entrance to Andrei's building.

The front door to the building wasn't locked. Once inside, Leah found that someone had conveniently propped the inner security door open with a large red brick. So Kay and Leah could go on up to Andrei's apartment without ringing the downstairs bell. But who, Leah wondered, would do such a thing?

"What does this open door mean?" Kay said meekly as she followed Leah up the dimly lit stairs to the third floor. "Do you think someone has broken in or something?"

"I don't know," Leah confessed, her heart pounding in her rib cage. "But we can't turn back now, whatever it is."

As Leah and Kay reached the second floor, the unmistakable sounds of a party somewhere in the

building reached them. The music and laughter
made Leah feel braver. And as the girls got closer
to the third floor, the party noises grew louder.
Finally, at the top of the stairs, Leah stopped.
"Good, the party's on this floor. That means there'll
be plenty of people around if we need help."

Kay smiled and nodded. Clearly the lively sounds
had put her at ease, too.

Still cautious, however, the girls continued slowly
down the hallway. Once they were standing in
front of Andrei's door, Kay cried, "The party's in
Andrei's apartment! Listen, Leah."

"You're right, that's the music James told me
they're using for *Temptations*! I bet Andrei is having a party for all the people who'll be in the
movie. They're going to start filming soon, you
know," Leah said excitedly, "so it makes perfect
sense." Suddenly, Leah smiled.

"What is it?" Kay asked. "What are you smiling
about?"

"James Cummings and Diana Chang are probably in there. And do you know who else?" Kay
shook her head. "I bet Alex is here, Kay!" Leah
cried, grabbing Kay's hands and giving them a
squeeze. "I bet Alex didn't come to the ballet
because she was getting ready for this party. You
know how fussy Alex is about the way she looks.
She just about went crazy at that dumb come-as-
you-are party! Remember? They're shooting *Temptations* around school. I bet old Alex was hoping
to get something more than just a walk-on part
by coming to Andrei's party looking her best. We
all know how worried she's been about her career lately."

"But what about all her missing clothes?" Kay

asked, not looking very convinced. "Why would Alex take all those clothes with her to a party?"

"Maybe Alex straightened up her closet today and took a bunch of stuff to the cleaners," Leah offered.

"Why would Andrei invite Alex and not you?" Kay pressed.

Leah shrugged. "I turned down the role of Cara Dean, remember? That kind of makes me a defector from the cast. Besides, Andrei probably felt sorry for Alex because of the whole Kirov thing. It certainly makes sense to me! Why, this party even explains why we couldn't find Andrei during intermission. He left the ballet early to set up his party."

Kay heaved a sigh of relief. "I hope you're right, Leah. But I hate to crash Andrei's party to find out for sure. If you *are* right, I'm going to feel really dumb."

"Andrei won't mind," Leah assured Kay, thinking of Andrei's warm smile and friendly eyes. "I know he likes us, both of us. I suppose he couldn't invite everyone up to his apartment for a party. It would be too crowded. Besides, we have to go in there to borrow money for the bus or a cab or something. He'll understand that. We can't get back to Mrs. Hanson's without Andrei's help, unless we want to walk."

"I certainly don't want to," Kay said. "I'm exhausted!"

Feeling confident, Leah took hold of the heavy brass knocker and rapped it against the door three times.

Instantly, the music within stopped and the friendly party sounds died. A few seconds later

Andrei's door slowly squeaked open and Andrei's boyish face appeared in the narrow crack.

It seemed to take a couple of seconds for Andrei to realize just who was outside his door. Then his eyes lit up. "Leah Stephenson!" he cried, opening the door just enough to squeeze out into the hall with them. "And little Kay Larkin!" Carefully, Andrei shut the door behind him. Then his look grew somber. "It is late! What are you thinking of to come this time of night?"

Leah smiled. "Come on, Andrei. We aren't dumb, you know. We could hear your party from downstairs, so don't try to pretend you aren't having one. We know Alex is in there, too. We'd like to talk to her for a minute and we also need to borrow bus fare back to the boardinghouse from one or the other of you. You might as well let us in."

"Alex?" Andrei repeated, looking confused. "I have party, yes. But Alex does not come," Andrei insisted, widening his stance and effectively barring the girls' entrance to his apartment.

"Look, Andrei," Leah said, raising her voice slightly. "Kay and I have been worried sick about Alex all week. We wouldn't be here now if it weren't for Alex, so the least you can do is let us in so we can see her!" With that, Leah pushed past Andrei.

"Andrei, who are these people?" Leah demanded, eyeing the sea of strange faces before her. Then she noticed the pile of wool coats on the floor by the door.

"It's the Russians!" Kay gasped before Leah could catch her breath long enough to speak.

"Andrei, where is Alex?" Leah asked, grabbing

Andrei's shoulders and giving him a shake. "What are these people doing here? They're not the *Temptations* crew!"

"No. These are old friends," Andrei said with a shrug.

"Friends!" Kay shrieked. "These people have kidnapped Alex and brainwashed her into returning to the Soviet Union. How can they be your friends?"

Andrei turned to the cluster of people standing in his living room and began talking to them in Russian. A few laughed at what Andrei was saying, but others of them looked angry. Finally, one of the women in the group pointed her finger at Leah and Kay and said something that sounded as if she thought *they'd* done something awful to *her*!

"What did Andrei say to them?" Kay asked Leah. "What did that woman say about us?"

"I don't know, Kay. Andrei," Leah said, pulling Andrei around so that he faced her once more, "what are you telling them?"

"I only repeat in Russian what you say to me about spies," Andrei answered, a silly grin on his face.

"What is wrong with American girls, Andrei?" the woman who'd spoken earlier asked. "Do all girls at this school hate Russian people? These girls follow *us*, as you warn might happen when we talk to you after ballet. They are being the spies, I think."

Leah's mouth dropped open as she finally recognized the woman who'd just spoken. She wasn't wearing much makeup at the moment, and her long hair was braided rather than pinned up in a tight chignon. But Leah still knew without a doubt that this was the woman who had danced the difficult dual role of Odette/Odile in the Kirov's performance of *Swan Lake* earlier that very evening. Leah recognized her beautiful arm movements. Even in anger her movements were those of the enchanted Swan Queen.

Andrei must have seen the recognition in Leah's eyes because he said, "Ah, now you see the truth, Leah. These people are no spies, they are my good friends from the Kirov Ballet! We party together tonight, for old time's sake."

Leah felt her face turn scarlet. There had to be at least twenty dancers from the Kirov in Andrei's apartment, and all of them were looking at Leah and Kay like they were insane.

"Oh, Andrei, what can I say to apologize?" Leah asked. "I feel awful. Please tell your friends that we don't think all Russians are bad. Tell them we're your friends, your good friends. It's just that we've been worried sick about Alex. If she isn't here with you, where is she?"

"What is all this about Alex?" Andrei asked, a worried scowl wrinkling his brow.

Taking a deep breath, Leah said, "Alex was supposed to meet us at the Opera House tonight. We were going to sneak her in, but she never showed up. When we got back to the boarding-house, we found nearly half of her clothes missing."

"Yes," Kay said, jumping in excitedly. "Remember what Madame Preston said last Sunday after class, Andrei? You know, about suspicious-looking people? Well, Leah and I have been watching very carefully and last Sunday on our way to the Asian Art Museum—"

"But, Kay," Leah interrupted. "That was a mistake, remember?"

Kay nodded, but she looked a little confused.

"I do not understand this," Andrei commented, looking as bewildered as Kay.

"That stuff at the Asian Art Museum was a false alarm," Leah tried to explain. "But I'll tell you something that is real," Leah promised. Then she told Andrei about the man from Cocoa-Nuts lurking outside Alex's window, and about the phone call. "And then that same man was at the ballet, sitting just a few seats from us. He even winked at me," Leah told him.

"Maybe you just have more false alarm," Andrei suggested.

"It's no false alarm," Kay said vehemently, her cheeks bright with anger. "Alex's clothes are gone and everything. The Russians have brainwashed her into giving up her freedom!"

"Brainwashed?" one of Andrei's guests repeated, lifting one eyebrow questioningly. "What is this washing of brain, Levintoff?"

Then everyone in the room began talking at once, mixing Russian and English in an excited-sounding jibberish.

"Quiet, quiet!" Andrei ordered, first in English and then in Russian. When the room was finally under control again, Andrei turned back to Leah. "I must understand what you say. Alex is missing, no?"

Leah nodded. "Yes!" Her eyes stung with the tears she feared would begin flowing at any moment, a result of the exhaustion and frustration she'd experienced that evening.

Andrei patted Leah comfortingly on the shoulder. "Why have you girls come to me?" he finally asked. "I do not know what I am to do for you."

"You defected," Kay said, "so we thought you'd understand the process. I mean, that's what we think Alex has done, only in reverse. What can we do to save her, Andrei?"

"Save Alex from Russia?" Andrei repeated skeptically. "Do you forget Alex *is* Russian?"

"What Kay means, Andrei, is that if Alex really wants to go back to Russia to live, that's her choice," Leah explained. "We just want to make sure that Alex really has had a choice, that's all. That's what we mean by brainwashing! We're afraid someone has convinced Alex that her life will be *better* in Russia than it is here in San Francisco. We aren't sure she has all the facts."

Andrei turned to his guests and said something in Russian. Then all his guests started putting on their dark green coats and fur-trimmed hats.

"My friends go. I do not want them in trouble. They go, then we call Madame and get to bottom of this thing."

After the last guest was gone, Andrei ushered Leah to his phone and gave her Madame Preston's home phone number. Meekly, Leah dialed.

"Hello?" said a sleepy voice, which Leah instantly recognized as Alicia Preston's.

"Madame? This is Leah Stephenson. I'm calling about Alexandra Sorokin. I'm afraid ... she's missing."

"Here," Andrei said, reaching for the phone. "I talk to Madame."

Once Andrei identified himself to Madame Preston, there was a slight pause. Then Andrei said, "Of course, Madame. We come right over!"

After Andrei had hung up the phone, he put a comforting arm around both girls. "Andrei worries, too," he told them. "But Madame Preston takes charge now. Alex will be found."

Chapter 12

*Leah looked across Madame's for-*mal parlor at Kay, hoping to catch her friend's eye. But Kay was absorbed in the steaming mug of hot chocolate Madame Preston had served her and the others after they'd arrived at her lovely Victorian house. So instead, Leah stared out the large bay windows.

During the day one could see San Francisco Bay from where Leah was sitting. But now Madame's heavy gold draperies were drawn against the dark night. Leah shivered slightly and tightened her grip on the warm mug she was holding.

"Would anyone care for a little ice cream?" Madame suddenly asked.

"No, thank you," Leah quickly replied.

"How about you, Katherine?" Madame asked, using Kay's full name.

Looking up from her mug nervously, Kay shook her head. Leah realized her friend hadn't been drinking the chocolate after all. She'd merely been staring into it, as if in a trance. Undoubtedly, Kay felt as tired as Leah did.

"And what about you, Andrei? Surely you will have some ice cream."

Andrea smiled. "Is it chocolate?" he asked.

Madame laughed. "Yes, as a matter of fact, it is chocolate!"

Andrei leapt to his feet. "I help you get it."

"No, no," Madame said. "Sit down. I will get it. You stay here with the girls. The others should be arriving any moment now."

As soon as Madame had left the room, Kay looked from Leah to Andrei and back again. Then she said, "How can you both be so calm? Something terrible has happened to Alex. I just know it. And it's all my fault, too!"

Leah set down her hot chocolate. "I'm just as worried as you are, Kay, believe me. But what more can we do? Madame's called the authorities. When they come, we'll tell them everything we know. We just have to hope, that's all."

Leah was about to say that Madame didn't seem very worried even though she had called her sister, Mrs. Hanson, to verify that Alex was not at the boardinghouse. But the sound of the doorbell stopped her. "That must be whoever Madame's been waiting for now," she said.

"Mr. Munroe," Leah heard Madame Preston say from the front hall a moment later. "How good of you to respond to my call so quickly."

"Mrs. Preston," Mr. Munroe replied, "I'd like you to meet a couple of associates of mine. This is Sergeant Pierce of the San Francisco Police Department, and this is Mr. Collins."

Leah waited to hear who Mr. Collins was associated with, but Mr. Munroe didn't say. As their footsteps came closer and closer to the parlor, Leah felt herself grow increasingly tense. Madame Preston entered first, followed by a man in a police uniform. Then Leah gasped as the next man walked into the room. There he was—the man who had been spying on Alex!

Leaping to her feet, Kay shrieked, "You caught him! You caught him!"

Madame looked startled. "Caught who, Katherine dear?"

"The KGB man! The one who's been tailing Alex. The man who was watching us at the Opera House! That man!" Kay finally concluded, pointing at the man from Cocoa-Nuts, who was still wearing the suit he'd had on at the ballet.

Leah couldn't stop staring at him. She knew she was being rude, but she couldn't help it. Yet, the man didn't seem the least upset, nor did he seem surprised to see Kay and Leah. In fact, he smiled at Leah just as he had at the Opera House earlier that evening.

"Girls, I'm afraid you've made a mistake. This is Mr. Munroe from the FBI," Madame Preston said calmly. "He *has* been watching Alex this week. But he was protecting her, not spying on her as you suggest. Unfortunately, there are some tricky political situations to be faced whenever a ballet company from the Soviet Union visits us. Fortunately, the good parts of their visits always outweigh any trouble we experience. I think I can safely say that the Soviets feel the same way."

Leah felt herself nodding. She felt like an idiot—an absolute, complete idiot. Now that she knew the man she'd seen lurking outside the boardinghouse was from the FBI, Leah was uncertain about *all* of her suspicions and conclusions. As Leah watched the three men sit down across from her, she couldn't help thinking of Clara in *The Nutcracker* awakening from her dream, wondering if the battle between the toy soldiers and the mice had really taken place at all. . . .

"Now, girls, I want you to tell us everything," Madame told them once the three men were comfortably seated.

Before Leah could decide where to begin, Kay started babbling about their bus trip to Golden Gate Park. "They were wearing sunglasses," Kay said, waving her arms frantically, "and it was cloudy!" Kay paused to catch her breath.

"But, Kay," Leah said, hoping to quiet her friend, "those people were the Kabuki lecturers at the Asian Art Museum. Remember?"

"Were they?" Kay demanded. "I mean, they did give a lecture, but that doesn't mean they weren't also spies. Well, anyway, we wanted Alex to go with us, but she said she had something else to do, although she never did say what. In fact, Alex has been acting strange all week," Kay raced on, sounding more and more excited with every word.

Listening to Kay recount all the things that had seemed to vitally important all week made Leah realize how silly they'd both been. Nothing of any real significance had happened other than the man who had been watching them. And now that he turned out to be an FBI agent, his presence didn't seem threatening at all.

Then Leah remembered the mysterious phone call. She waited for a good moment to break into Kay's hysterical discourse. "There was *one* other thing," she said when Kay had stopped explaining the museum incident. "After I saw you out in front of the boardinghouse, Mr. Munroe, Alex got a phone call. I thought it was you, but now I know it wasn't you after all."

"What time was this?" Sergeant Pierce asked, getting ready to add to his notes.

"I'm not sure," Leah answered carefully. "I didn't actually look at a clock or anything. But I'd been on my way home from the library, which closes at ten. It was probably close to ten-thirty, maybe a little later. Of course, I did watch Mr. Munroe watching Alex for a while."

"What did the man say?" Mr. Collins asked, leaning forward in his chair and looking sternly at Leah. Of the three men, Mr. Collins was the most intimidating to Leah. He was wearing a black three-piece suit and a dark tie; he looked as if he meant business. Next to him, Mr. Munroe looked downright pleasant.

Taking a deep breath, Leah said, "Well, he asked for Alex. I told him she was in bed already, so he said I was to give Alex a message. He said she should meet him at three o'clock. When I asked where, he said she already knew where. That's what made me think Alex might be planning on going back to Russia."

"Going back!" Mr. Collins bellowed, frightening Leah.

Mr. Munroe looked at Mr. Collins and shook his head. Then turning to Leah, he said, "Did this caller have a Russian accent, then?"

"You said he did, Leah," Kay blurted out.

Leah shook her head. "He didn't, and then he did. I mean, it seemed like the more he said, the more I could tell he had an accent. I mean ..." Leah let her voice trail off as she shook her head again. She wasn't sure of anything anymore.

"And you called your sister's house after the

girls here called you, right?" Sergeant Pierce asked Madame.

"Yes, I called her while I was waiting for Andrei and the girls to arrive. My sister checked, and Alexandra was not in her room," Madame replied. "I am quite concerned."

Getting to his feet, Mr. Munroe said, "Well, I think the girls have told us everything they have to tell. Right, girls?" Leah and Kay nodded. "We'll take it from here, then."

"Will you see that the girls get home, Andrei?" Madame asked. Andrei nodded. Then, getting to his feet, he took both girls' hands and guided them toward the front door.

"We walk," Andrei said. "It is a short distance from here."

Andrei was just about to open the door when Mr. Collins covered Andrei's hand with his. "That was a pretty reckless stunt you pulled, Levintoff. Having a party like that at your place."

Andrei smiled sheepishly and shrugged. "Sometimes I am reckless," he said.

"Just don't think we didn't notice, that's all," Mr. Collins said, then he removed his hand from Andrei's and took a step back. Andrei opened the door and ushered the girls outside.

"Who was that Mr. Collins?" Kay asked.

Andrei shrugged again. "He is like Russian KGB only American, a bully. Anyway, is nothing more to be done now. We all go to bed. Tomorrow, I think, we have answers."

"I certainly hope you're right, Andrei," Leah said, pulling up the collar of her wool coat against the damp night air.

*   *   *

Leah sat down against the wall of the Red Studio and watched the marzipans mark their waltz steps together. Tchaikovsky's lovely music was like a lullaby, tempting Leah to get the sleep she'd failed to get the night before.

Leah had been able to sleep only a couple of hours. It had been nearly two o'clock by the time Andrei delivered her and Kay to Mrs. Hanson, who had shooed the girls up to their rooms before they'd had a chance to thank Andrei. Leah also wanted to apologize again for ruining his party and getting him into trouble with Mr. Collins.

Tired as she'd been, Leah hadn't been able to go right to sleep. She'd still been worried about Alex, even though the fate of her friend was out of her hands. Leah had tried to tell herself that Mr. Munroe and Mr. Collins were professionals; but somehow that made her worry even more.

Naturally, Alex's safe return had been the first thought in Leah's head upon waking the next morning. But after dressing quickly and dashing down to the second floor, Leah had discovered that Alex's bed had not been slept in. Alex was still missing!

Alex had not showed up for their Saturday morning class, and now she was conspicuously absent from the afternoon *Nutcracker* rehearsal. Leah didn't know what to think.

She didn't want to do anything to make Madame any angrier at her than Leah was afraid Madame already was. Somehow, Leah had managed to get through the class with Madame that morning. Leah had been afraid that Madame would point out the errors Leah felt she was making because she was weak from lack of sleep. But

Madame had kindly ignored both Leah and Kay during class.

Unfortunately, Madame Preston was now going over the divertissements from the last act of *The Nutcracker* with the students, while Patrick watched from his perch on a tall metal stool. Leah suspected that she wasn't out of hot water yet as she grimly forced her eyelids to remain open. Madame, Leah was afraid, was just waiting until Alex was found before she lowered the boom on her and Kay.

Madame was demonstrating the marzipans' port de bras when her secretary burst into the studio and ran across the wooden floor, her high heels making a loud, clattering noise. Madame lowered her arms and looked questioningly at the intruder. Everyone, including Madame's secretary, knew that street shoes were forbidden in the studios.

"Phone call, Madame," the secretary said loudly enough so Leah could hear her. "It's urgent!"

Madame motioned for Patrick to take over, and then she followed her secretary out of the studio without saying a word.

It had to be Alex! Leah told herself joyfully. Finally, someone had found her. But was Alex all right, she wondered anxiously.

Rehearsal continued as Patrick finished with the marzipans and called the coffee dancers forward. Only Kay, sitting in a chair that was serving as Clara's throne for this rehearsal, seemed to be as worried as Leah.

Suddenly, just when Leah thought she would go out of her mind with worry, Madame Preston swept back into the room. After a quick consultation with Patrick, Madame dismissed the coffee dancers and recalled the marzipans, asking them to dance their little waltz full out for her. Then Madame signaled the accompanist to begin playing the marzipan waltz.

All the while, Leah kept her eyes glued on Madame. She longed for some kind of sign, any kind of sign, from Madame. Surely, Leah told herself, the phone call had to have concerned Alex. And Madame was well aware of the fact that Leah and Kay were dying to know the status of their missing friend!

Then, just as the marzipans began to dance, Madame looked across the studio. As soon as her eyes met Leah's, Madame Preston smiled. Leah felt as if she'd just seen sunlight for the first time in days. Madame's smile could mean only one thing, Leah told herself. Alex had been found, and she was all right!

Chapter 13

"*Madame Preston smiled at me!*" Leah whispered delightedly to Kay as the girls hurried to the dressing room after *The Nutcracker* rehearsal.

Kay gave Leah's arm an excited squeeze. "Madame smiled at me, too! I think Alex must be okay. Don't you?"

Leah nodded. "Maybe Alex is even back at the boardinghouse this very minute, waiting to tell us her whole exciting story."

"What are you two so worked up about?" Pam demanded, suddenly appearing behind Kay and Leah in the hall outside the dressing room.

Leah forced herself to stand a little straighter as she said, "Nothing important, Pam."

"Humpf!" Pam snorted indignantly. Then the fiery redhead stormed past them into the dressing room.

"Let's go back to Mrs. Hanson's right now, Leah, and see if Alex is there," Kay suggested as soon as the door had slammed safely shut behind Pam.

"You mean not go in the dressing room?" Leah asked.

"If we go in there, everyone will just start asking us a lot of questions like they did last night and again this morning. I'm not in the mood for that, especially since I don't really know anything more than I did before."

"I agree. Let Alex tell them her story if she wants to." But Leah hesitated, thinking of her overworked muscles and the drizzly December day, a disastrous combination for a dancer's body. "The only problem is I've got some things in the dressing room, like my denim jacket. I don't want to get chilled and pull a muscle or something."

"Here," Kay said, pulling a sweater from her dance bag. "You can use this. I've got another one in my bag I can use. We'll run. I'm too eager to find out about Alex to worry about getting cold."

"I can't wait until this whole mess is over, either!" Leah agreed, pulling the sweater over her black leotard, which was still damp from rehearsal.

The girls walked quickly down the second floor hallway toward the stairway to the first floor. They were about to start down the stairs when out of the corner of her eye Leah spotted a few people sitting outside of Madame Preston's office.

"Kay, look!" Leah cried, stopping as she realized who it was. "That's Alex down at the end of the hall outside Madame's office door, isn't it?"

"You're right! She's with Mrs. Hanson ... and someone else I don't recognize," Kay exclaimed. "Come on! Let's go talk to her!"

But Leah didn't move. She squinted in an effort to see more clearly beyond the patch of sunlight coming through the window at the far end of the hall. "I think that's Mrs. Lydgate."

"I wonder what *she's* doing here," Kay mused.

"Come on, Leah. Let's go ask Alex what's going on."

But before the girls could get close enough to get Alex's attention without shouting, Madame Preston's door opened and her secretary ushered everyone outside into Madame's office.

"Oh, well," Kay said, still smiling. "At least we know for sure that Alex is okay. Let's go back to Mrs. Hanson's. We can shower and have something to eat before she gets back. I bet she's got a whopper of a story for us, too." With that, Kay charged down the stairs.

Leah hurried after Kay. Now that she knew Alex was all right, Leah couldn't help feeling sort of angry with her Russian friend. Alex, Leah told herself, better have an *awfully* good story—a story worth all the worry Leah and Kay had experienced the last several days.

"How can you even think of eating all that?" Leah demanded as the girls started up to the second floor of the boardinghouse with sandwiches they'd just finished making for themselves.

"You had it easy this afternoon," Kay told her. "You just had to do your little dance with the other Polichinelles, then you got to sit back and watch. I had to be Clara every second, all afternoon!"

Leah shook her head. She didn't have much sympathy for Kay's plight of having to dance the best part in *The Nutcracker*. "Do you want me to feel sorry for you because you get to dance Clara?" Leah asked.

Kay laughed. "Of course not. I love being Clara. Rehearsal just made me hungry, that's all."

The girls were about to go into Kay's room to

eat their sandwiches when Leah noticed that Alex's door was slightly ajar. "That's funny. Alex's door is open," she told Kay. "It was shut tight this morning when I came downstairs."

"Maybe Alex got back while we were in the kitchen!" Kay cried, turning around and heading straight for Alex's room.

But no one answered when Leah knocked on the door. "I guess she's not back yet," Leah said, trying to peer into the brightly decorated room through the narrow slit created by the slightly open door.

"Nonsense," Kay said dismissively as she stepped in front of Leah. "You didn't knock hard enough, that's all." Kay struck Alex's door sharply with her fist, and the door swung open. Kay shrugged. "Her door's open now. We may as well go in and wait for her."

Leah hesitated. When she'd feared that something awful had happened to Alex, it had seemed perfectly all right to go into her room while she wasn't there. But now that Alex appeared to be safe and sound, Leah felt uncomfortable about trespassing. "I'm not sure we should."

"Why not? We went in there last night. We even looked through her closet," Kay countered.

"That was different," Leah insisted. "We thought Alex was in danger."

"Well, I'm going in to wait for her. I've been through too much this past week to risk missing her," Kay said. "I need a good night's sleep for a change, and I know I'm not going to get it until I've heard her whole story from start to finish."

Leah had to agree on that point, and she followed Kay into the room.

She was looking for somewhere to sit when she noticed a thick bouquet of brilliant red roses on Alex's dresser. Leaning against the vase was a small envelope. Unable to resist checking it out, Leah set her sandwich down on Alex's desk and crossed the room.

"Oh!" Kay squealed, noticing the flowers just as Leah reached the note. "Who could those be from?"

"I don't know," Leah said, "but I'm about to find out." Picking up the small envelope and pulling out the tiny card, Leah read out loud, " 'All my love, Ben.' "

"Ben?" Kay repeated. "Ben who?"

"Ben Lydgate," a husky voice with a decidedly Russian accent answered.

Leah spun around and, just as she'd feared, found herself face-to-face with Alexandra. Scowling angrily, Alex snatched the card from Leah. "This, I think, is mine. What are you two doing in my room, anyway? *Spying?*" Alex arched her eyebrows emphatically.

"I ... I ..." Leah began.

Then Kay broke in with "We ... we ..."

But before either Leah or Kay could finish saying anything, Alex suddenly doubled over with laughter. When she'd finally calmed down enough to speak, she said, "Madame Preston told me the whole story. How you two thought I was going to be kidnapped so that my parents would be forced to return to Russia. Then, when you saw me on the phone more often than usual, you jumped to the conclusion that I was plotting to return to Russia to dance with the Kirov Ballet." Once again Alex broke into gales of laughter.

"It is too funny. You girls have much too much

imagination, I think, even for dancers. Imagination is good when it lets you believe in the part you are performing onstage. But it is a bad thing when it causes you to distort reality like this. I can see Kay doing this. Kay has it in mind to be a choreographer and design dances, create movement. But you, Leah! I would have expected you to have more sense!"

"But you were missing," Kay insisted. "You've been gone since Friday afternoon! If the Russians didn't have you, then who were you with?"

"Ben Lydgate!" Leah answered for Alex. Then, turning to Alex, Leah said, "You *have* been with Ben Lydgate, haven't you, Alex? Ben Lydgate is the man I talked to on Thursday night. You met him Friday at three o'clock, didn't you?"

Kicking off her narrow black ankle boots, Alex flopped lazily down on her brightly colored bedspread. "You are not such a bad detective after all, Leah Stephenson. What you have just said is true."

"How could you do that to us?" Leah demanded.

"To you?" Alex countered. "I was not aware of doing anything to you. Ben was only disguising his voice so you would not recognize it. He did not mean to scare you. Whatever did or didn't happen to the two of you is only of your own making."

Kay gasped. "How can you say that, Alex? Leah and I have been so worried, we put ourselves in a lot of danger because of you."

"As it turns out, we weren't really in any danger," Leah amended. "But we didn't know that at the time. We were willing to put ourselves in grave danger for you, Alex, because we thought you were our friend. But now I know differently. Now I know you laugh at our friendship."

"You never told me your worries, did you?" Alex countered, starting to chuckle again. "You just watched me and made up stories to explain what you saw instead of asking me to explain."

"We got you tickets to the Kirov," Leah reminded Alex, feeling increasingly put out by Alex's carefree attitude. "We waited outside for you until it was nearly curtain time. Then we worried about you through the whole ballet. I can't speak for Kay, but I can barely remember what the dancing was like. All I could do was worry about you. Those tickets were expensive, and who knows when the Kirov will be in San Francisco again. Besides, I *did* ask you who was on the phone once, and you refused to tell me! After the funny way you've been acting lately, I didn't want to press the issue with you."

Hugging an orange throw pillow to her chest, Alex smiled mysteriously and said, "Don't you want to know where I went with Ben Lydgate?"

"No!" Leah said firmly.

"I do," Kay said eagerly, ignoring Leah. "Where were you?"

"I went to Oregon to Ben's college for their Winter Wonderland Weekend," Alex answered, falling back dreamily on her bed. She didn't seem the least bit interested in placating Leah.

Leah wanted to storm out of Alex's room, but she couldn't make herself. As much as she hated to admit it, she was just as eager as Kay to hear Alexandra's story.

"How was it?" Kay asked, sitting on the edge of Alex's bed, one foot tucked beneath her.

Alex's grin reminded Leah of the Cheshire cat in *Alice's Adventures in Wonderland.* "It was wonderful! It was the best time I have ever had in my life!"

"A college weekend!" Leah exclaimed. "How can you say that about a college weekend?"

Alex winked at Kay, then turned to Leah. "Have you ever *been* to a college weekend?" she asked.

"Well, no," Leah admitted, feeling angrier by the minute. As far as she was concerned, Alex was acting totally ridiculous. Leah found it hard to believe that this was the same girl who Leah had once thought of as her best friend, the same girl who had won the Golden Gate Award for being a dancer of exceptional promise. Alex was acting like a silly schoolgirl, not a professional dancer.

"Then you cannot know," Alex sighed, putting her hands behind her head and continuing to stare up at the ceiling dreamily. "There was a dance and I, Alexandra Sorokin, was crowned Queen of the Snow! Many people tell me that I am beautiful!"

"Really?" Kay said appreciatively. "Did you get to wear a crown?"

"A beautiful crown," Alex said, sitting up again and wrapping her arms around her legs. "I was permitted to keep the crown, too. I will show it to you when I unpack."

"Why didn't you just tell us you were going away, Alex?" Leah asked. "Why did you leave us thinking you were going to meet us at the Opera House? I think if I had done something like that to you, you would never want to speak to me again."

Suddenly Alex looked serious. "You are right,

Leah. That was a bad thing to do. I am sorry, but I had to fool you. If you knew, you would have had to tell Madame what you knew or you would have gotten into trouble. Going away without permission is forbidden, you know. You would have been punished if you had known and not told, just as you were punished once for knowing about James Cummings's injury and not telling Madame. I did think of that, and I was trying to protect you. Now I am on probation for the rest of the year. I know you would not want such a thing, either one of you."

Kay nodded. "Alex is right, you know, Leah. Besides, if you really think about it, we did have an awfully exciting week."

"I can live without that kind of excitement," Leah assured Kay. "And we got into trouble anyway. We were up until two o'clock in the morning last night, sitting in Madame Preston's house being interviewed by the FBI. We ruined Andrei's party with his Kirov friends. And to top it off, we were scared out of our wits—about you!"

Alex burst out laughing again.

"Now what's so funny?" Leah asked, folding her arms across her chest. "I really don't think this is funny."

"Oh, but it is, it really is! I was just thinking that maybe I would be better off, you know, more free, in the Soviet Union after all," Alex said, still chuckling slightly. "Maybe I should have told you. But I didn't know that you would do what you did. I had no idea all that nonsense would happen. At the time, not telling you seemed like the right thing to do."

"What about your parents?" Leah asked. "Aren't

they going to be furious when they find out about this?"

"They already know," Alex replied. "I talked to my mother about going and she gave her permission on the condition that I ask Madame Preston first. I did ask Madame—but she said no, absolutely not."

"And you went anyway?" Kay gasped.

"My mother said only that I needed to *ask* Madame, you see. She never said Madame had to say it was all right for me to go." Alex giggled. "Anyway," she went on, "Madame's reason for forbidding me to go was that it was too dangerous for me to go anywhere with the Soviets in San Francisco," Alex explained. "You can see what little sense that made. If the Soviets were making San Francisco dangerous for me, was it not safer for me to leave town?"

"That does make sense, doesn't it?" Kay asked, turning to Leah.

Leah shrugged. "About as much sense as any of this makes to me, I guess," she admitted.

"So I did save you from getting into the same kind of trouble I'm in," Alex said, grinning again. "You're not on probation like I am. I think that Madame will not punish you anymore. From the sound of your story, I would say you have punished yourselves quite enough." The silly grin returned to Alex's lips. Clearly, Alex was unable to keep a serious look on her face for long.

"Well, I'm glad someone around here was able to have a good time," Leah finally said as she retrieved her sandwich from Alex's desk and headed for the door. Leah felt she'd heard enough for now. Alex might not have defected from the

United States, but Leah had a strong feeling that Alex might well be in the process of defecting from the world of dance.

Leaping off the bed, Alex pirouetted across the room and back again. "Is no one going to ask me about Ben?" Alex declared, collapsing on her bed once more.

Kay laughed. "What about Ben, Alex?"

"He's just ... great. All I can say is that I am in love. Alexandra Sorokin is finally in love!"

Kay smiled dreamily, but Leah could not. Maybe, Leah told herself, she should feel happy for Alex. After all, this was just what Alex wanted.

But something told Leah that this wasn't the happy ending Alex seemed to think it was. What was going to happen to Alex's dancing career now that she was in love? She was already on probation; if she missed any more important rehearsals, Alex might get kicked out of the Academy.

For the moment Leah was just glad that her friend was safe, however. Leah didn't know what would happen to Alex next, but one thing was for sure—she wouldn't be going to the Soviet Union!

GLOSSARY

Adagio. Slow tempo dance steps; essential to sustaining controlled body line. When dancing with a partner, the term refers to support of ballerina.

Allegro. Quick, lively dance step.

Arabesque. Dancer stands on one leg and extends the other leg straight back while holding the arms in graceful positions.

> *Arabesque penchée.* The dancer's whole body leans forward over the supporting leg. (Also referred to as penché.)

Assemblé. A jump in which the two feet are brought together in the air before the dancer lands on the ground in fifth position.

Attitude turns. The *attitude* is a classical position in which the working or raised leg is bent at the knee and extended to the back, as if wrapped around the dancer. An *attitude turn* is a turn performed in this position.

Balloon. Illusion of suspending in air.

Barre. The wooden bar along the wall of every ballet studio. Work at the barre makes up the first part of practice.

Battement. Throwing the leg as high as possible into the air to the front, the side, and the back. Several variations.

> *Battement en cloche.* Swinging the leg as high as possible to the back and to the front to loosen the hip joint.

Batterie. A series of movements in which the feet are beaten together.

> *Grande batterie.* Refers to steps with high elevation.

> *Petite batterie.* Steps with small elevation.

Bourrée. Small, quick steps usually done on toes. Many variations.

Brisé. A jump off one foot in which the legs are beaten together in the air.

Centre work. The main part of practice; performing steps on the floor after barre work.

Chaîné. A series of short, usually fast turns on pointe by which a dancer moves across the stage.

Corps de ballet. Any and all members of the ballet who are not soloists.

Dégagé. Extension with toe pointed in preparation for a ballet step.

Developpé. The slow raising and unfolding of one leg until it is high in the air (usually done in pas de deux, or with support of barre or partner).

Divertissement. A series of entertaining and/or technically brilliant dances performed within a ballet. For example, as in the Marzipan dance of *The Nutcracker* or in the Bluebird Variation in the last act of *Sleeping Beauty*.

Echappé. A movement in which the dancer springs up from fifth position onto pointe in second position. Also a jump.

Enchaînement. A sequence of two or more steps.

Entrechat. A spring into the air from the fifth position in which the extended legs (with feet well pointed) criss-cross at the lower calf.

Fouetté. A step in which the dancer is on one leg and uses the other leg in a sort of whipping movement to help the body turn.

Frappé (or *battement frappé*). A barre exercise in which the dancer extends the foot of the working leg to the front, side and back, striking the ball of the foot on the ground. Dancer then stretches the toe until it is slightly off the ground and returns the foot *sur le cou-de-pieds* (on the ankle) against the ankle of the supporting leg.

Glissade. A gliding step across the floor.

Jeté. A jump from one foot onto the other in which the working leg appears to be thrown in the air.

Jeté en tournant. A jeté performed while turning.

Mazurka. A Polish national dance.

Pas de deux. Dance for 2 dancers. ("Pas de trois" means dance for 3 dancers, and so on.)

Pas de chat. Meaning "step of the cat." A light, springing movement. The dancer jumps and draws one foot up to the knee of the opposite leg, then draws up the other leg, one after the other, traveling diagonally across the stage.

Penché. Referring to an arabesque penchée.

Piqué. Direct step onto pointe without bending the knee of the working leg.

Plié. With feet and legs turned out, a movement by which the dancer bends both knees outward over her toes, leaving her heels on the ground.

Demi plié. Bending the knees as far as possible leaving the heels on the floor.

Grand plié. Bending knees all the way down letting the heels come off the floor (except in second position).

Pointe work. Exercises performed in pointe (toe) shoes.

Port de bras. Position of the dancer's arms.

Posé. Stepping onto pointe with a straight leg.

Positions. There are five basic positions of the feet and arms that all ballet dancers must learn.

Rétiré. Drawing the toe of one foot to the opposite knee.

Rond de jambe à terre. An exercise performed at the barre to loosen the hip joint: performed first outward (*en dehors*) and then inward (*en dedans*). The working leg is extended first to the front with the foot fully pointed and then swept around to the side and back and through first position to the front again. The movement is then reversed, starting from the fourth position back and sweeping around to the side and front. (The foot traces the shape of the letter "D" on the floor.)

Sissonne. With a slight plié, dancer springs into the air from the fifth position, and lands on one foot with a demi plié with the other leg extended to the back, front, or side. The foot of the extended leg is then closed to the supporting foot.

Tendu. Stretching or holding a certain position or movement.

Tour en l'air. A spectacular jump in which the dancer leaps directly upwards and turns one, two, or three times before landing.

Here's a look at what's ahead in CHANCE TO LOVE, the ninth book in Fawcett's "Satin Slippers" series for GIRLS ONLY.

"I think it's time to go," Leah said reluctantly when there was a lull in the conversation. "We've got another class that I don't want to miss."

"You certainly are dedicated," Peter said admiringly. Leah was relieved that he didn't try to talk her out of going to her next class. Instead, he got up and ran to pay the bill, insisting that Leah wait for him so he could walk her back.

"Are you coming, Alex?" Leah asked once Peter had left the table.

Alex shook her head. "Ben must leave for school tomorrow, early. We have planned to spend the afternoon together."

Leah had to bite her tongue to keep from saying something. She knew Alex was making a mistake. She was already in a lot of trouble at school without adding to it by skipping classes. But Alex was a big girl, Leah told herself. She could make her own decisions.

When Peter got back to the table, he said good-bye to Alex and Ben, adding that he hoped to see them both again soon. Then, taking Leah's hand again, he walked her outside.

"You don't need to walk the rest of the way with me," Leah told him once they were outside. "In fact, I see a bus coming now. Maybe you should take it back to school."

Peter shook his head. "No way! I promised to bring you back to the Academy and I'm a man of my word.

Besides, you promised to show me this famous ice-cream place."

Hearing Peter call himself a man made Leah giggle. "All right then, Mr. Forrest," she joked. "Come on, I'll give you the dancer's tour of the SFBA neighborhood."

Peter nodded as he slipped his hands into the pockets of his red-and-white letter jacket. "Great! I'm anxious to see just where it is you spend your time."

"Why?" Leah asked.

"So that when I'm not with you, I can imagine where you are."

"That's sweet," Leah told him.

"Not really. It's just practical," Peter reassured her.

"And where will you be when I'm not with you?" Leah asked, playing along.

"At Manzanita High," he replied.

"I've been there," she said. "I can imagine that. Where else?"

"Shooting baskets at the park with some guys I know," he told her. Leah couldn't help laughing.

"What's so funny?" Peter demanded.

"I should have known you were a basketball player," Leah said, still smiling.

"Why? Because I'm so tall?"

Leah felt herself blush. "I guess that's stereotyping. I'm sorry."

It was Peter's turn to laugh. "Sorry but right! I am a basketball player. Actually, I got into basketball before I knew that I was going to be tall. I'm lucky, really."

"I feel lucky too. Some girls who love ballet have to give it up because their bodies grow wrong. So far, that hasn't happened to me," Leah concluded.

"Hey," Peter cried, pointing at the sign hanging between the two stone pillars that guarded the long driveway leading up the Victorian mansion that housed the San Francisco Ballet Academy. "Here we are, and you never pointed out that place to me."

Leah laughed. "I'm sorry. I guess I was so busy talking I forgot all about conducting a tour. Next time," she added.

But Leah's warm smile turned cold as she saw Madame's silver car approaching the gate from the opposite direction. Suddenly, Leah realized that what had started out as an innocent walk home had turned into a date of sorts. Leah stepped in front of Peter as if doing so would hide his six foot frame from Madame.

As Madame's car swept past them, through the gate and up the drive, Peter tapped Leah on the shoulder. "What's going on?" he asked, his bright green eyes clouding slightly. "Who was in that car?"

"It was nothing, I mean, no one," Leah insisted, quickly deciding that there was no way to gracefully explain her fear of Madame Preston's disapproval of dating to Peter. Besides, Leah wasn't sure that Peter thought of their time together as a date anyway. Looking up at Peter's good-natured face, Leah felt she wasn't sure anymore about much of anything.

One thing she did know, though. Getting involved with someone was the last thing Leah wanted. Being with Peter this afternoon had seemed so natural, so easy—but she didn't have time for him. She'd already had to skip one class just to see him for an hour or so.

"I've got to be going," Leah told him abruptly. "I'm going to be late as it is." She turned and started to hurry up the driveway.

"Wait!" Peter called after her. "I want your phone number. Peggy wants your phone number, too."

But Leah didn't wait. She liked Peter, but she couldn't let him call her. She couldn't fall for Peter Forrest the way Alex had fallen for Ben Lyndgate. Madame Preston, Leah knew, would simply not stand for it.

ABOUT THE AUTHOR

ELIZABETH BERNARD has had a lifelong passion for dance. Her interest and background in ballet is wide and various and has led to many friendships and acquaintances in the ballet and dance world. Through these connections she has had the opportunity to witness firsthand a behind-the-scenes world of dance seldom seen by non-dancers. She is familiar with the stuff of ballet life: the artistry, the dedication, the fierce competition, the heartaches, the pains, and disappointments. She is the author of over a dozen books for young adults, including titles in the bestselling COUPLES series, published by Scholastic, and the SISTERS series, published by Fawcett.